A to Z Mysteries
COLLECTION #1

COLLECTION #1

by Ron Roy

illustrated by
John Steven Gurney

A STEPPING STONE BOOK™

Random House 🏠 New York

The Absent Author
Text copyright © 1997 by Ron Roy
Cover art copyright © 2015 by Stephen Gilpin
Interior illustrations copyright © 1997 by John Steven Gurney

The Bald Bandit
Text copyright © 1997 by Ron Roy
Cover art copyright © 2015 by Stephen Gilpin
Interior illustrations copyright © 1997 by John Steven Gurney

The Canary Caper
Text copyright © 1998 by Ron Roy
Cover art copyright © 2015 by Stephen Gilpin
Interior illustrations copyright © 1998 by John Steven Gurney

The Deadly Dungeon
Text copyright © 1998 by Ron Roy
Cover art copyright © 2015 by Stephen Gilpin
Interior illustrations copyright © 1998 by John Steven Gurney

All rights reserved. Published in the United States by Random House Children's Books, a division of Penguin Random House LLC, New York.

Random House and the colophon and A to Z Mysteries are registered trademarks and A Stepping Stone Book and the colophon and the A to Z Mysteries colophon are trademarks of Penguin Random House LLC.

Visit us on the Web!
SteppingStonesBooks.com
randomhousekids.com

Educators and librarians, for a variety of teaching tools, visit us at
RHTeachersLibrarians.com

Library of Congress Cataloging-in-Publication Data for these titles is available upon request.

The Absent Author
ISBN 978-0-679-88168-1 (trade) — ISBN 978-0-679-98168-8 (lib. bdg.) — ISBN 978-0-307-51012-9 (ebook)

The Bald Bandit
ISBN 978-0-679-88449-1 (trade) — ISBN 978-0-679-98449-8 (lib. bdg.) — ISBN 978-0-307-51373-1 (ebook)

The Canary Caper
ISBN 978-0-679-88593-1 (trade) — ISBN 978-0-679-98593-8 (lib. bdg.) — ISBN 978-0-307-51642-8 (ebook)

The Deadly Dungeon
ISBN 978-0-679-88755-3 (trade) — ISBN 978-0-679-98755-0 (lib. bdg.) — ISBN 978-0-307-51961-0 (ebook)

Printed in the United States of America   20 19 18 17 16 15 14 13

These books have been officially leveled by using the F&P Text Level Gradient™ Leveling System.

Random House Children's Books supports the First Amendment and celebrates the right to read.

Contents

A to Z Mysteries™

The Absent Author

by **Ron Roy**

illustrated by
John Steven Gurney

A STEPPING STONE BOOK™

Random House New York

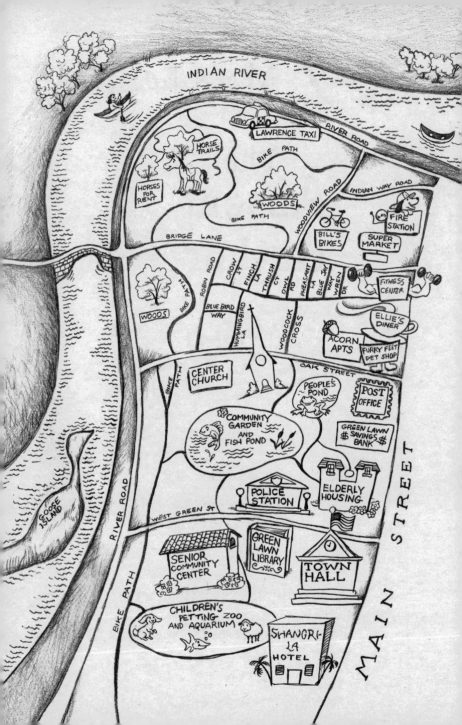

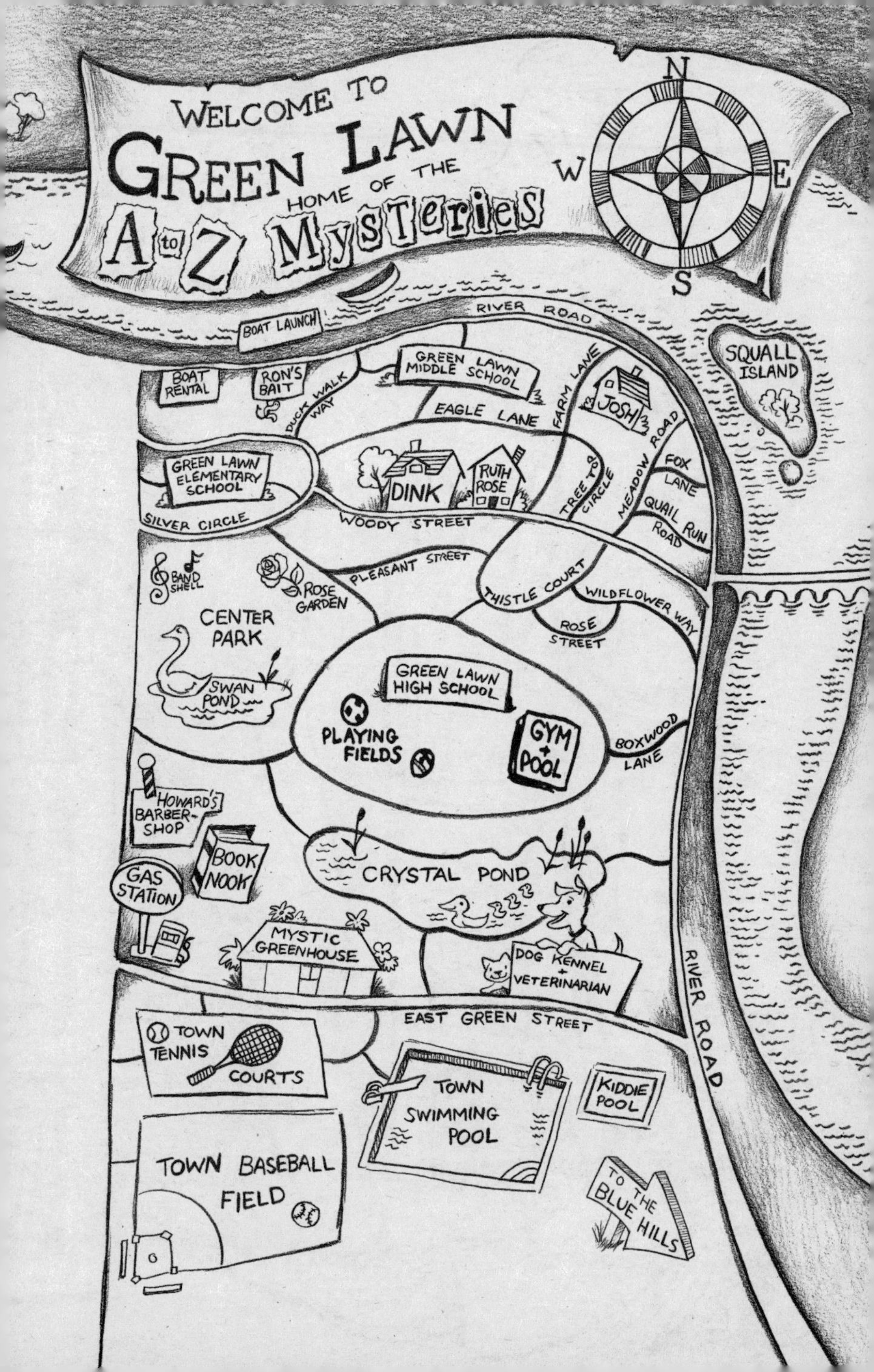
WELCOME TO
GREEN LAWN
HOME OF THE
A to Z MysTeries
N
W
E
S
RIVER ROAD
BOAT LAUNCH
SQUALL ISLAND
BOAT RENTAL
RON'S BAIT
DUCK WALK WAY
GREEN LAWN MIDDLE SCHOOL
EAGLE LANE
FARM LANE
JOSH
MEADOW ROAD
GREEN LAWN ELEMENTARY SCHOOL
DINK
RUTH ROSE
TREE TOP CIRCLE
FOX LANE
QUAIL RUN ROAD
SILVER CIRCLE
WOODY STREET
BAND SHELL
ROSE GARDEN
PLEASANT STREET
THISTLE COURT
WILDFLOWER WAY
ROSE STREET
CENTER PARK
SWAN POND
GREEN LAWN HIGH SCHOOL
PLAYING FIELDS
GYM + POOL
BOXWOOD LANE
HOWARD'S BARBER-SHOP
BOOK NOOK
GAS STATION
CRYSTAL POND
MYSTIC GREENHOUSE
DOG KENNEL + VETERINARIAN
RIVER ROAD
EAST GREEN STREET
TOWN TENNIS COURTS
TOWN SWIMMING POOL
KIDDIE POOL
TOWN BASEBALL FIELD
TO THE BLUE HILLS

Chapter 1

"Please, Josh," Dink said. "If you come with me today, I'll owe you one. Just name it. *Anything!*"

Dink's full name was Donald David Duncan. But no one in Green Lawn ever called him that. Except his mother, when she meant business.

Josh Pinto grinned at his best friend.

"Anything?" He raised his mischievous green eyes toward the ceiling of Dink's bedroom. "Let's see, what do you have that I want?" He scratched his head. "I know, I'll take Loretta!"

Dink tossed a pillow at Josh. "When I said *anything,* I meant anything but my guinea pig! Are you coming with me or not? I have to be at the Book Nook in fifteen minutes!"

Dink rushed into the bathroom, tucking his shirt into his jeans at the same time. Josh followed him.

Standing in front of the mirror, Dink yanked a brush through his thick blond hair. "Well?" he asked. "Are you coming with me?"

"What's so important about this writer guy?" Josh asked, sitting on the edge of the bathtub.

Dink turned around and pointed his hairbrush. "Wallis Wallace isn't just

some writer guy, Josh. He's the most famous mystery writer in the world! All the kids read his books. Except for you."

"If he's so famous, why's he coming to dinky little Green Lawn?"

Dink charged back into his bedroom. "I told you! He's coming because I *invited* him. I'm scared to death to meet someone so famous. I don't even know what you're supposed to say to an author!"

Dink dived under his bed and backed out again with his sneakers. "Please come with me?"

Josh leaned in the bedroom doorway. "Sure I'll come, you dope. I'm just trying to make you sweat. Usually you're so calm!"

Dink stared at his friend. "You will? Thanks! I can't believe Wallis Wallace is really coming. When I wrote and asked him, I never thought he'd say yes."

Dink yanked his backpack out of his closet. "Pack my books, okay? I'm getting Wallis Wallace to sign them all!"

Josh began pulling Wallis Wallace books off Dink's bookshelf. "Geez, how many do you have?"

"Every one he's written." Dink sat on the floor to tie his sneakers. "Twenty-three so far. You should read some of them, Josh."

Josh picked out *The Poisoned Pond* and read the back cover. "Hey, cool! It says here that Wallis Wallace lives in a castle in Maine! Wouldn't that be neat?"

Dink grinned. "When I'm a famous writer, you can live in my castle, Josh."

"No way. When I'm a famous *artist*, you can live in *my* castle. Down in the basement!"

Josh picked up *The Riddle in the River.* "What's this guy look like?" he

asked. "And how come his picture isn't on any of these books?"

"I wondered about that, too," Dink said. "I sent him one of my school pictures and asked for one of him. But when I got his letter, there was no picture."

He finished tying his laces. "Maybe Wallis Wallace just doesn't like having his picture taken."

Josh squeezed all twenty-three books into Dink's pack. He grinned at Dink. "Or maybe he's just too ugly."

Dink laughed. "Gee, Josh, *you're* ugly and you love having your picture taken."

"Haw, haw." Josh picked up his drawing pad. "But just because you're my best friend, I'll draw his picture at the bookstore."

Dink looked at his watch. "Yikes!" he said. "We have to pick up Ruth Rose in one minute!" He tore into the bathroom and started brushing his teeth.

"How'd you get her to come?" Josh called.

Dink rushed back into his room, wiping toothpaste from his mouth. "You kidding? Ruth Rose loves Wallis Wallace's books."

Dink slung his backpack over his shoulder. He and Josh hurried next door to 24 Woody Street. Tiger, Ruth Rose's orange cat, was sitting in the sun on the steps.

Dink pressed the doorbell.

Ruth Rose showed up at the door.

As usual, she was dressed all in one color. Today it was purple. She wore purple coveralls over a purple shirt and had on purple running shoes. A purple baseball cap kept her black curls out of her face.

"Hey," she said. Then she turned

around and screamed into the house. "THE GUYS ARE HERE, MOM. I'M LEAVING!"

Dink and Josh covered their ears.

"Geez, Ruth Rose," Josh said. "I don't know what's louder, your outfit or your voice."

Ruth Rose smiled sweetly at Josh.

"I can't wait until Wallis Wallace signs my book!" she said. She held up a copy of *The Phantom in the Pharmacy.*

"I wonder if Wallis Wallace will read from the new book he's working on," Dink said.

"What's the title?" Ruth Rose asked.

They headed toward the Book Nook.

"I don't know," said Dink. "But he wrote in his letter that he's doing some of the research while he's here in Connecticut."

Dink pulled the letter out of his

pocket. He read it out loud while he walked.

W

Dear Mr. Duncan,

Thank you for your kind letter. I'm so impressed that you've read all my books! I have good news. I've made arrangements to come to the Book Nook to sign books. I can use part of my time for research. Thanks for your picture. I'm so happy to finally meet one of my most loyal fans. Short of being kidnapped, nothing will stop me from coming!

See you soon,

Wallis Wallace

The letter was signed *Wallis Wallace* in loopy letters. Dink grinned. "Pretty neat, huh?"

"Pretty neat, *Mister* Duncan!" teased Josh.

"You should have that letter framed," Ruth Rose said.

"Great idea!" Dink said.

They passed Howard's Barbershop. Howard waved through his window as they hurried by.

"Come on!" Dink urged as he dragged his friends down the street to the Book Nook.

They looked through the window, out of breath. The bookstore was crowded with kids. The Book Nook's owner, Mr. Paskey, had set up folding chairs. Dink noticed that most of them were already taken.

Dink saw Mr. Paskey sitting behind a table. A big white sign on the table said WELCOME, WALLIS WALLACE!

But the chair behind the sign was empty. Dink gulped and stared at the empty seat.

Where was Wallis Wallace?

Chapter 2

Dink raced into the Book Nook. Josh and Ruth Rose were right behind him. They found three seats behind Tommy Tomko and Eddie Carini.

Dink plopped his pack on the floor. The clock over the cash register said three minutes after eleven.

"Where is he?" Dink whispered to Tommy Tomko.

Tommy turned around. "Beats me. He's not here yet, and Mr. Paskey looks worried."

"What's going on?" Ruth Rose said.

11

Dink told her and Josh what Tommy had said.

"Paskey does look pretty nervous," Josh whispered.

"Mr. Paskey always looks nervous," Dink whispered back, looking around the room. He saw about thirty kids he knew. Mrs. Davis, Dink's neighbor, was looking at gardening books.

Dink checked out the other grownups in the store. None of them looked like a famous mystery writer.

Mr. Paskey stood up. "Boys and girls, welcome to the Book Nook! Wallis Wallace should be here any second. How many of you have books to be autographed?"

Everyone waved a book in the air.

"Wonderful! I'm sure Wallis Wallace will be happy to know that Green Lawn is a reading town!"

The kids clapped and cheered.

Dink glanced at the clock. Five past eleven. He swallowed, trying to stay calm. Wallis Wallace was late, but it was only by five minutes.

Slowly, five more minutes passed. Dink felt his palms getting damp. *Where* is *Wallis Wallace?* he wondered.

Some of the kids started getting restless. Dink heard one kid say, "Whenever *I'm* late, I get grounded!"

"So where is he?" Josh asked.

Ruth Rose looked at her watch. "It's only ten after," she said. "Famous people are always late."

Now Dink stared at the clock. The big hand jerked forward, paused, then wobbled forward again.

At 11:15, Mr. Paskey stood up again. "I don't understand why Wallis Wallace is late," he said. Dink noticed that his bald head was shiny with sweat. His bow tie was getting a workout.

Mr. Paskey smiled bravely, but his eyes were blinking like crazy through his thick glasses. "Shall we give him a few more minutes?"

The crowd grumbled, but nobody wanted to go anywhere.

Ruth Rose started to read her book.

Josh opened his sketch pad and began drawing Mr. Paskey. Dink turned and stared at the door. He mentally ordered Wallis Wallace to walk through it. *You have to come!* thought Dink.

Ever since he had received Wallis Wallace's letter, he'd thought about only one thing: meeting him today.

Suddenly Dink felt his heart skip a beat. THE LETTER! *Short of being kidnapped,* the letter said, *nothing will stop me from coming.*

Kidnapped! Dink shook himself. Of course Wallis Wallace hadn't been kidnapped!

Mr. Paskey stood again, but this time he wasn't smiling. "I'm sorry, kids," he said. "But Wallis Wallace doesn't seem to be coming after all."

The kids groaned. They got up, scraping chairs and bumping knees. Mr. Paskey apologized to them as they crowded past, heading for the door.

"I've read every single one of his books," Dink heard Amy Flower tell another girl. "Now I'll probably *never* meet anyone famous!"

"I can't believe we gave up a soccer game for this!" Tommy Tomko muttered to Eddie Carini on their way out.

Ruth Rose and Josh went next, but Dink remained in his seat. He was too stunned to move.

He felt the letter through his jeans. *Short of being kidnapped...* Finally Dink got up and walked out.

Josh and Ruth Rose were waiting for him.

"What's the matter?" Ruth Rose said. "You look sick!"

"I *am* sick," Dink mumbled. "I invited him here. It's all my fault."

"What's all your fault?" Josh asked.

"This!" he said, thrusting the letter into Josh's hands. "Wallis Wallace has been *kidnapped!*"

Chapter 3

"KIDNAPPED?" Ruth Rose shrieked. Her blue eyes were huge.

Josh and Dink covered their ears.

"Shh!" said Josh. He handed the letter back to Dink and gave a quick gesture with his head. "Some strange woman is watching us!"

Dink had noticed the woman earlier. She'd been sitting in the back of the Book Nook.

"She's coming over here!" Ruth Rose said.

The woman had brown hair up in a neat bun. Half-glasses perched on her nose. She was wearing a brown dress and brown shoes, and carried a book bag with a picture of a moose on the side. Around her neck she wore a red scarf covered with tiny black letters.

"Excuse me," she said in a soft, trembly voice. "Did you say Wallis Wallace has been *kidnapped?*" The woman poked her glasses nervously.

Dink wasn't sure what to say. He *thought* Wallis Wallace had been kidnapped, but he couldn't be sure. Finally he said, "Well, he might have been."

"My goodness!" gasped the woman.

"Who are you?" Josh asked her.

"Oh, pardon me!" The woman blushed. "My name is Mavis Green," she mumbled. "I'm a writer, and I came to meet Mr. Wallace."

Dink said, "I'm Dink Duncan. These are my friends Ruth Rose and Josh."

Mavis shook hands shyly.

Then she reached into her book bag and pulled out a folded paper.

"Wallis Wallace wrote to me last week. He said something very peculiar in his letter. I didn't think much of it at the time. But when he didn't show up today, and then I heard you mention kidnapping..."

She handed the letter to Dink. Josh and Ruth Rose read it over his shoulder.

Dear Mavis,

Thanks for your note. I'm well, and thank you for asking. But lately my imagination is playing tricks on me. I keep thinking I'm being followed! Maybe that's what happens to mystery writers—we start seeing bad guys in the shadows! At any rate, I'm eager to meet you in Green Lawn, and I look forward to our lunch after the signing.

Wallis Wallace

"Wow!" said Ruth Rose. "First he says he's being followed, and then he winds up missing!"

Dink told Mavis about his letter from Wallis Wallace. "He said the only thing that would keep him from coming today was if he was kidnapped!"

"Oh, dear!" said Mavis. "I just don't understand. Why would anyone want to kidnap Wallis Wallace?"

"If he's the most famous mystery writer in the world, he must be rich, right?" Josh said. "Maybe someone kid-napped him for a ransom!"

Suddenly Josh grabbed Dink and spun him around, pointing toward the street. "Look! The cops are coming! They must have heard about the kid-napping!"

A police officer was walking toward them.

"Josh, that's just Officer Fallon,

Jimmy Fallon's grandfather," said Dink. "Jimmy came to get a book signed. I saw him inside the Book Nook."

"Maybe we should show Officer Fallon these letters," Ruth Rose suggested. "They could be clues if Wallis Wallace has really been kidnapped!"

"Who's been kidnapped?" asked Officer Fallon, who was now standing near them. "Not my grandson, I hope," he added, grinning.

Dink showed Officer Fallon the two letters. "We think Wallis Wallace might have been kidnapped," he said. "He promised he'd come to sign books, but he isn't here."

Officer Fallon read Mavis's letter first, then Dink's. He scratched his chin, then handed the letters back.

"The letters do sound a bit suspicious," he said. "But it's more likely that Mr. Wallace just missed his flight."

Jimmy Fallon ran out of the Book Nook, waving a Wallis Wallace book at his grandfather. "Grampa, he never came! Can we go for ice cream anyway?"

Officer Fallon put a big hand on Jimmy's head. "In a minute, son." To Dink he said, "I wouldn't worry. Mr. Wallace will turn up. Call me tomorrow if there's no news, okay?"

They watched Jimmy and his grandfather walk away.

Dink handed Mavis's letter back to her. He folded his and slid it into his pocket. Crazy thoughts were bouncing around in his head. *What if Wallis Wallace really has been kidnapped? It happened because I invited him to Green Lawn. I'm practically an accomplice!*

"I don't want to wait till tomorrow," he said finally. "I say we start looking for Wallis Wallace now!"

"Where do we start?" Ruth Rose asked.

Dink jerked his thumb over his shoulder. "Right here at the Book Nook."

"Excuse me," Mavis Green said shyly. "May I come along, too?"

"Sure," Dink said. He marched back inside the Book Nook, with the others following.

Mr. Paskey was putting the Wallis Wallace books back on a shelf. He looked even more nervous than before.

"Excuse me, Mr. Paskey," Dink said. "Have you heard from Wallis Wallace?"

Mr. Paskey's hand shot up to his bow tie. "No, Dink, not a word."

"We think he was kidnapped!" Josh said.

Mr. Paskey swallowed, making his bow tie wiggle. "Now, Joshua, let's not jump to conclusions. I'm sure there's a rational explanation for his absence."

Dink told Mr. Paskey about the two letters. "I'm really worried, Mr. Paskey. Where could he be?"

Mr. Paskey took out a handkerchief and wiped his face. "I have no idea." He removed a paper from his desk and handed it to Dink. "All I have is his itinerary."

The others looked over Dink's shoulder as he read:

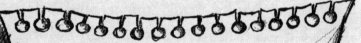

Itinerary for Wallis Wallace:

1. Arrive at Bradley Airport at 7:00 P.M., Friday, July 15, New England Airlines, Flight 3132.

2. Meet driver from Lawrence Taxi Service.

3. Drive to Shangri-La Hotel.

4. Sign books at Book Nook at 11:00 A.M., Saturday, July 16.

5. Lunch, then back to airport for 4:30 P.M. flight.

"Can I keep this?" Dink asked Mr. Paskey.

Mr. Paskey blinked. "Well, I guess that'll be all right. But why do you need the itinerary?"

Dink picked up a marker and drew circles around the words AIRPORT, TAXI, HOTEL, and BOOK NOOK.

"This is like a trail. It leads from the airport last night to the Book Nook today," Dink said. "Somewhere along this trail, Wallis Wallace disappeared."

Dink stared at the itinerary. "And we're going to find him!"

Chapter 4

Mr. Paskey shooed them out of the Book Nook and locked the front door. "I have to eat lunch," he said. He scurried down Main Street.

"Come on," Dink said. "There's a phone in Ellie's Diner."

"Good, we can eat while you're calling..." Josh stopped. "Who are you calling?"

"The airport," Dink said, "to see if Wallis Wallace was on that seven o'clock flight last night."

They walked into Ellie's Diner just

as Jimmy Fallon and his grandfather came out. Jimmy was working on a triple-decker chocolate cone.

Ellie stood behind the counter. As usual, her apron was smeared with ketchup, mustard, chocolate, and a lot of stuff Dink didn't recognize.

Ellie smiled. "Hi, Dink. Butter crunch, right?"

Dink shook his head. "No, thanks, Ellie. I came to use the phone."

"Excuse me, but would it be all right if I bought you each a cone?" Mavis Green asked. "I was going to buy lunch for Mr. Wallace anyway."

"Gee, thanks," Josh said. "I'll have a scoop of mint chip and a scoop of pistachio."

"Oh, you like green ice cream, too," Mavis said. She smiled shyly. "I'll have the same, please."

"I like pink ice cream," Ruth Rose

said. "I'll have a strawberry cone, please. One scoop."

"How about you, Dink?" Mavis asked.

"I'm not hungry, thanks," he said. "But you guys go ahead. I'm going to call the airport."

Dink felt guilty. If he hadn't invited Wallis Wallace to Green Lawn, his favorite author would be safe at home in his castle in Maine.

But Dink couldn't help feeling excited too. He felt like a detective from one of Wallis Wallace's books!

Dink stepped into the phone booth, looked up the number for New England Airlines, and called. When a voice came on, he asked if Wallis Wallace had been aboard Flight 3132 last night.

"He was? Did it land at seven o'clock?" Dink asked. "Thanks a lot!"

He rushed out of the phone booth. "Hey, guys, they told me Wallis Wallace was on the plane—and it landed right on time!"

"So he didn't miss his flight," Ruth Rose said through strawberry-pink lips.

"That's right!" Dink pulled out the itinerary. He drew a line through AIR-PORT.

"This is so exciting!" Ruth Rose said.

"Now what?" Josh asked, working on his double-dipper.

Dink pointed to his next circle on the itinerary. "Now we need to find out if a taxi picked him up," he said.

"Lawrence Taxi is over by the river," Ruth Rose said.

Dink looked at Mavis. "Would you like to come with us? We can walk there in five minutes."

Mavis Green wiped her lips carefully with a napkin. "I'd love to come," she said in her soft voice.

They left Ellie's Diner, walked left on Bridge Lane, then headed down Woodview Road toward the river.

"Mr. Paskey looked pretty upset, didn't he?" Josh said, crunching the last of his cone. His chin was green.

"Wouldn't you be upset if you had a bunch of customers at your store waiting to meet a famous author and he didn't show up?" Ruth Rose asked.

"Yeah, but he was sweating buckets," Josh said. "I wonder if Mr. Paskey kidnapped Wallis Wallace."

"Josh, get real! Why would Mr.

Paskey kidnap an author?" asked Ruth Rose. "He sells tons of Wallis Wallace's books!"

"I don't think Mr. Paskey is the kidnapper," Dink said. "But in a way, Josh is right. Detectives should consider everyone a suspect, just the way they do in Wallis Wallace's books."

At River Road, they turned left. Two minutes later, Dink pushed open the door of the Lawrence Taxi Service office. He asked the man behind the counter if one of their drivers had met Flight 3132 at Bradley Airport the previous night.

The man ran his finger down a list on a clipboard. "That would be Maureen Higgins. She's out back eating her lunch," he said, pointing over his shoulder. "Walk straight through."

They cut through the building to a grassy area in back. Through the trees,

Dink could see the Indian River. The sun reflected off the water like bright coins.

A woman was sitting at a picnic table eating a sandwich and filling in a crossword puzzle.

"Excuse me, are you Maureen Higgins?" Dink asked.

The woman shook her head without looking up. "Nope, I'm Marilyn Monroe."

The woman wrote in another letter. Then she looked up. She had the merriest blue eyes Dink had ever seen.

"Yeah, cutie pie, I'm Maureen." She pointed her sandwich at Dink. "And who might you be?"

"I'm Dink Duncan," he said. "These are my friends Josh, Ruth Rose, and Mavis."

"We wondered if you could help us," Ruth Rose said.

Maureen stared at them. "How?"

"Did you pick up a man named Wallis Wallace at the airport last night?" Dink asked.

Maureen squinted one of her blue eyes. "Why do you want to know?"

"Because he's missing!" said Josh.

"Well, I sure ain't got him!" Maureen took a bite out of her sandwich. Mayonnaise oozed onto her fingers.

"I know. I mean, we didn't think you had him," Dink said. "But did you pick him up?"

Maureen nodded, swallowing. "Sure I picked him up. Seven o'clock sharp, I was there with my sign saying WALLACE. The guy spots me, trots over, I take him out to my taxi. He climbs in, carrying a small suitcase. Kinda spooky guy. Dressed in a hat, long raincoat, sunglasses. Sunglasses at night! Doesn't speak a word, just sits. Spooky!"

"Did you take him to the Shangri-la Hotel?" Dink asked.

"Yep. Those were my orders. Guy didn't have to give directions, but it woulda been nice if he'd said something. Pass the time, you know? Lotta people, they chat just to act friendly. Not this one. Quiet as a mouse in the back seat."

Maureen wiped mayonnaise from her fingers and lips. "Who is this Wallace fella, anyway?"

"He's a famous writer!" Ruth Rose said.

Maureen's mouth fell open. "You mean I had a celebrity in my cab and never even knew it?"

"What happened when you got to the hotel?" Josh asked.

Maureen stood up and tossed her napkin into the trash. "I get out of my side, then I open his door. He hops out,

hands me a twenty. Last I seen, he's scooting into the lobby."

Dink pulled out the itinerary. He crossed out TAXI with a thick black line. Then he drew a question mark next to HOTEL.

"Thanks a lot, Miss Higgins," he said. "Come on, guys, I have a feeling we're getting closer to finding Wallis Wallace."

Maureen put her hand on Dink's arm. "I just thought of something," she said. "When he handed me my fare, this Wallace fella was smiling."

Dink stared at Maureen. "Smiling?"

She nodded. "Yep. Had a silly grin on his face. Like he knew some big secret or something."

Back on Main Street, Dink adjusted his backpack and led the way to the Shangri-la Hotel.

"Maureen Higgins said she dropped him off at the hotel last night," he told the others, "so that's our next stop."

"What if she didn't?" Josh said, catching up to Dink.

"What do you mean?"

"I mean maybe Maureen Higgins wasn't telling the truth. Maybe *she* kidnapped him!"

"And she's hiding him in her lunch-

box!" Ruth Rose said.

"Very funny, Ruth Rose," Josh said. "Maureen Higgins said she drove Wallis Wallace to the hotel. But what if she drove him somewhere else?"

"You could be right," Dink said. "That's why we're going to the hotel."

With Dink in the lead, the four approached the check-in counter in the hotel lobby.

"Excuse me," Dink said to the man behind the counter.

"May we help you?" He was the saddest-looking man Dink had ever seen. He had thin black hair and droopy eyebrows. His skinny mustache looked like a sleeping centipede. A name tag on his suit coat said MR. LINKLETTER.

"We're looking for someone."

Mr. Linkletter stared at Dink.

"He's supposed to be staying in this hotel," Josh said.

The man twitched his mustache at Josh.

"His name is Wallis Wallace," Dink explained. "Can you tell us if he checked in last night?"

Mr. Linkletter patted his mustache. "Young sir, if we had such a guest, we wouldn't give out any information. We have *rules* at the Shangri-la," he added in a deep, sad voice.

"But he's missing!" Ruth Rose said. "He was supposed to be at the Book Nook this morning and he never showed up!"

Dink pulled out the itinerary. "See, he was coming here from the airport. The taxi driver said she saw him walk into this lobby."

"And he's famous!" Ruth Rose said. She placed her book on the counter in front of Mr. Linkletter. "He wrote this!"

Sighing, Mr. Linkletter looked down

at Ruth Rose. "We are quite aware of who Mr. Wallace is, young miss."

Mr. Linkletter turned his sad eyes back on Dink. He flipped through the hotel register, glanced at it, then quickly shut the book. "Yes, Mr. Wallace checked in," he said. "He arrived at 8:05."

"He did? What happened after that?" Dink asked.

Mr. Linkletter pointed toward a bank of elevators. "He went to his room. We offered to have his suitcase carried, but he preferred to do it himself."

"Have you seen Mr. Wallace yet today?" Mavis asked.

"No, madam, I haven't seen him. Mr. Wallace is still in his room."

Still in his room!

Suddenly Dink felt relieved. He felt a little foolish, too. Wallis Wallace hadn't been kidnapped after all. He was probably in his room right now!

"Can you call him?" Dink asked.

Mr. Linkletter tapped his fingers on the closed hotel register. He patted his mustache and squinted his eyes at Dink.

"Please?" Dink said. "We just want to make sure he's okay."

Finally Mr. Linkletter turned around. He stepped a few feet away and picked up a red telephone.

As soon as his back was turned, Josh grabbed the hotel register. He quickly found yesterday's page. Dink and the others crowded around Josh for a peek.

Dink immediately recognized Wallis Wallace's signature, scrawled in big loopy letters. He had checked in to Room 303 at five after eight last night.

Dink pulled out his letter from Wallis Wallace and compared the two

signatures. They were exactly the same.

Josh dug his elbow into Dink's side. "Look!" he whispered.

Josh was pointing at the next line in the register. ROOM 302 had been printed there. Check-in time was 8:15.

"Someone else checked in right after

Wallis Wallace!" Ruth Rose whispered.

"But the signature is all smudged," Dink said. "I can't read the name."

When Mr. Linkletter hung up the phone, Josh shoved the register away.

As Mr. Linkletter turned back around, Dink shut the register. He looked up innocently. "Is he in his room?" Dink asked.

"I don't know." Mr. Linkletter tapped his fingers on his mustache. "There was no answer."

Dink's stomach dropped. His mind raced.

If Wallis Wallace had checked into his room last night, why hadn't he shown up at the Book Nook today?

And why wasn't he answering his phone?

Maybe Wallis Wallace had been kidnapped after all!

Chapter 6

Dink stared at Mr. Linkletter. "No answer? Are you sure?"

Mr. Linkletter nodded. He looked puzzled. "Perhaps he's resting and doesn't want to be disturbed."

"Can we go up and see?" Ruth Rose smiled sweetly at Mr. Linkletter. "Then we'd know for sure."

Mr. Linkletter shook his head. "We cannot disturb our guests, young miss. We have *rules* at the Shangri-la. Now good day, and thank you."

Ruth Rose opened her mouth. "But, Mis—"

"Good day," Mr. Linkletter said firmly again.

Dink and the others walked toward the door.

"Something smells fishy," muttered Dink.

"Yeah," Josh said, "and I think it's that Linkletter guy. See how he tried to hide the register? Then he turned his back. Maybe he didn't even call Room 303. Maybe he was warning his partners in crime!"

"What are you suggesting, Josh?" Mavis asked.

"Maybe Mr. Linkletter is the kidnapper," Josh said. "He was the last one to see Wallis Wallace."

A man wearing a red cap tapped Dink on the shoulder. "Excuse me, but I overheard you talking to my boss, Mr.

Linkletter. Maybe I can help you find Wallis Wallace. My kids love his books."

"Great!" Dink said. "Can you get us into his room?"

The man shook his head. "No, but I know the maid who cleaned the third-floor rooms this morning. Maybe she noticed something."

With his back to Mr. Linkletter, the man scribbled a few words on a pad and handed the page to Dink. "Good luck!" the man whispered, and hurried away.

"What'd he write?" Josh asked.

"Outside," Dink said.

They all shoved through the revolving door. In front of the hotel, Dink looked at the piece of paper. "The maid's name is Olivia Nugent. She lives at the Acorn Apartments, Number Four."

"Livvy Nugent? I know her!" Ruth Rose said. "She used to be my baby-sitter."

"The Acorn is right around the corner on Oak Street," Dink said. "Let's go!"

Soon all four were standing in front of Livvy Nugent's door. She answered it with a baby in her arms. Another little kid held on to her leg and stared at Dink and the others. He had peanut butter all over his face and in his hair.

"Hi," the boy's mother said. "I'm not buying any cookies and I already get the *Green Lawn Gazette*." She was wearing a man's blue shirt and jeans. Her brown hair stuck out from under a Yankees baseball cap.

"Livvy, it's me!" Ruth Rose said.

Olivia stared at Ruth Rose, then broke into a grin.

"Ruth Rose, you're so big! What are

you up to these days?"

"A man at the hotel gave us your name."

"What man?"

"He was sort of old, wearing a red cap," Dink said.

Livvy chuckled. "Freddy old? He's only thirty! So why did he send you to see me?"

"He told us you cleaned the rooms on the third floor this morning," Dink said. "Did you clean Room 303?"

Livvy Nugent shifted the baby to her other arm. "Randy, please stop pulling on Mommy's leg. Why don't you go finish your lunch?" Randy ran back into the apartment.

"No," Livvy told Dink. "Nobody slept in that room. The bed was still made this morning. The towels were still clean and dry. I remember because there were two rooms in a row that I

didn't have to clean—303 and 302. Room 302 had a Do Not Disturb sign hanging on the doorknob. So I came home early, paid off the baby-sitter, and made our lunches."

"But Mr. Linkletter told us Wallis

Wallace checked into Room 303 last night," Ruth Rose said.

"Not *the* Wallis Wallace? The mystery writer? My kid sister *devours* his books!"

Dink nodded. "He was supposed to sign books at the Book Nook this morning. But he never showed up!"

"We even saw his signature on the hotel register," Ruth Rose said.

"Well, Wallis Wallace might have signed in, but he never slept in that room." Livvy grinned. "Unless he's a ghost."

"I wonder if Mr. Linkletter could have made a mistake about the room number," Mavis suggested quietly.

Livvy smiled at Mavis. "You must not be from around here. Mr. Linkletter *never* makes mistakes."

"So Wallis Wallace signed in, but he didn't sleep in his room," said Dink.

"That means..."

"Someone must have kidnapped him before he went to bed!" Josh said.

Livvy's eyes bugged. "Kidnapped! Geez, Mr. Linkletter will have a fit." She imitated his voice. "We have *rules* about kidnappings at the Shangri-la!"

Everyone except Dink laughed. All he could think about was Wallis Wallace, his favorite author, kidnapped.

Suddenly a crash came from inside the apartment. "Oops, gotta run," Livvy said. "Randy is playing bulldozer with his baby sister's stroller again. I hope you find Wallis Wallace. My kid sister will die if he doesn't write another book!"

They walked slowly back to Main Street. Dink felt as though his brain was spinning around inside his head.

Now he felt certain that Wallis Wallace had been kidnapped.

But who did it? And when?

And where was Wallis Wallace being kept?

"Guys, I'm feeling confused," he said. "Can we just sit somewhere and go over the facts again?"

"Good idea," Josh said. "I always think better when I'm eating."

"I'm feeling a bit peckish, too," Mavis said. "I need a quiet cup of tea and a sandwich. Should we meet again after lunch?"

Ruth Rose looked at her watch. "Let's meet at two o'clock."

"Where?" Josh asked.

"Back at the hotel." Dink peered through the door glass at Mr. Linkletter.

"Unless Maureen Higgins and Mr. Linkletter are *both* lying," he said, "Wallis Wallace walked into the Shangri-la last night—and never came out."

Dink, Josh, and Ruth Rose left Mavis at
Ellie's Diner, then headed for Dink's
house. Dink made tuna sandwiches and
lemonade. Ruth Rose brought a bag of
potato chips and some raisin cookies
from her house next door.

They ate at the picnic table in Dink's
backyard. Dink took a bite of his sandwich. After he swallowed, he said,
"Let's go over what we know."

He moved his lemonade glass to the
middle of the table. "My glass is the air-

port," he said. "We know Wallis Wallace landed."

"How do we *know* he did?" Josh asked.

"The airport told me the plane landed, Josh."

"And Maureen Higgins said she picked him up," Ruth Rose added.

"Okay, so your glass is the airport," Josh said. "Keep going, Dink."

Dink slid his sandwich plate over next to his glass. "My plate is Maureen's taxi." He put a cookie on the plate. "The cookie is Wallis Wallace getting into the taxi."

Dink slid the plate over to the opened potato chip bag. "This bag is the hotel." He walked the Wallis Wallace cookie from the plate into the bag.

Dink looked at Josh and Ruth Rose. "But what happened to Wallis Wallace after he walked into the lobby?"

"I'll tell you what happened," Josh said. He lined up four cookies in a row. "This little cookie is Mr. Paskey. These three are Maureen, Mr. Linkletter, and Olivia Nugent."

Josh looked up and waggled his eyebrows. "I think these four cookies planned the kidnapping *together!*"

Ruth Rose laughed. "Josh, Mr. Paskey and Livvy Nugent are friends of ours. Do you really think they planned this big kidnapping? And can you see Mr. Linkletter and my baby-sitter pulling off a kidnapping together?"

Josh ate a potato chip. "Well, maybe not. But *someone* kidnapped the guy!"

"Our trail led us to the hotel, and then it ended," Dink said. "What I want to know is, if Wallis Wallace isn't in his room, where is he?"

Dink nibbled on a cookie thoughtfully. "I'm getting a headache trying to sort it all out."

Ruth Rose dug in Dink's backpack and brought out three Wallis Wallace books. "I have an idea." She handed books to Dink and Josh and kept one.

"What're these for?" Dink asked.

"Josh made me think of something Wallis Wallace wrote in *The Mystery in the Museum*," Ruth Rose said. "He said the more you know about the victim, the easier it is to figure out who did the crime."

She turned to the back cover of her book. "So let's try to find out more about our victim. Listen to this." She started reading out loud. "'When not writing, the author likes to work in the garden. Naturally, Wallis Wallace's favorite color is green.'"

"Fine," said Josh, "but how does knowing his favorite color help us find him, Ruth Rose?"

"I don't know, but maybe if we read more about him, we'll discover some clues," Ruth Rose said. "What does it say on the back of your book?"

Josh flipped the book over and began

reading. "'Wallis Wallace lives in a castle called Moose Manor.'" He looked up. "We already knew he lived in a castle. I don't see any clues yet, you guys."

Ruth Rose stared at Josh. "You know, something is bugging me, but I can't figure out what it is. Something someone said today, maybe." She shook her head. "Anyway, read yours, Dink."

Dink read from the back cover of his book. "'Wallis Wallace gives money from writing books to help preserve the wild animals that live in Maine.'"

"Okay, he gives money away to save animals, lives in a castle, and grows a bunch of green stuff," Josh said, counting on his fingers. "Still no clues."

Josh took another cookie. "But I just thought of something." He began slowly munching on the cookie.

Dink raised his eyebrows. "Are you going to tell us, Josh?"

"Well, I was thinking about Room 302. Remember, someone signed the register right after Wallis Wallace checked into Room 303? And the signature was all smudged? And then Olivia Nugent—"

"—told us that Room 302 had a Do Not Disturb sign on it!" Ruth Rose interrupted. "Livvy never went into that room at all!"

Just then Dink's mother drove up the driveway. She got out of the car, waved, and started walking toward the picnic table.

"Oh, no!" Dink said. "If Mom finds out I'm trying to find a kidnapper, she won't let me out of the house! Don't say anything, okay?"

"Can't I even say hi?" Josh asked.

Dink threw a potato chip at Josh. "Say hi, then shut up about you-know-what!"

"Hi, Mrs. Duncan!" Josh said, sliding a look at Dink.

"Hi, kids. How was the book signing? Tell me all about Wallis Wallace, Dink. Is he as wonderful as you expected?"

Dink stared at his mother. He didn't want to lie. But if he told her the truth, she wouldn't let him keep looking for Wallis Wallace. And Dink had a sudden feeling that they were very close to finding him.

We can't stop now! he thought. He looked at his mother and grinned stupidly.

"Dink? Honey? Why is your mouth open?"

He closed his mouth. *Think, Dink!* he ordered himself.

Suddenly Josh knocked over his lemonade glass. The sticky cold liquid spilled into Dink's lap.

Dink let out a yowl and jumped up.

"Gee, sorry!" said Josh.

"Paper towels to the rescue!" Dink's mother ran toward the house.

"Good thinking, Josh," Dink said, wiping at his wet jeans. "But did you have to spill it on *me?* You had the whole yard!"

Josh grinned. "Some people are never satisfied. I got you out of hot water, didn't I?"

"Right into cold lemonade," Ruth Rose said.

Dink blotted his jeans with a handful of paper napkins. "Come on. Let's go meet Mavis before my mom comes back. There's something weird happening on the third floor of the Shangri-la!"

Chapter 8

Dink's jeans were nearly dry by the time they reached the hotel. Mavis was waiting out front.

"How was your lunch?" she asked timidly.

"Fine, thanks," Dink said. "We talked it over, and we think there's something fishy going on on the third floor of this hotel."

Suddenly Mavis began coughing. She held up her scarf in front of her mouth.

Dink noticed that the letters on the

scarf were tiny M's. "Are you okay?" he asked.

"Should I run in and get you some water?" asked Josh.

Mavis took off her glasses and shook her head. "No, I'm fine, thank you. Dear me, I don't know what happened! Now, what were you saying about the third floor?"

"We think Wallis Wallace may be up there," Ruth Rose said. She reminded Mavis about the smudged signature for Room 302 and the Do Not Disturb sign on the door.

Mavis replaced her eyeglasses. "Mercy! What do you think we should do?"

"Follow me!" Dink said. For the second time, they all trooped into the hotel lobby.

Mr. Linkletter watched them from behind the counter.

"Hi," Dink said. "Remember us?"

"Vividly," Mr. Linkletter said.

"Wallis Wallace checked into Room 303, right?"

"That is correct," said Mr. Linkletter.

"Well, we talked to the maid who cleaned that room," Dink went on. "She told us no one slept in it."

"You spoke to Olivia Nugent? When? How?"

"We have our ways," Josh said.

"So," Dink went on, "we think Wallis Wallace disappeared right here in this hotel."

"And Wallis Wallace is a *very* famous writer," Ruth Rose reminded Mr. Linkletter. "Millions of kids are waiting to read his next book," she added sweetly.

Mr. Linkletter's sad eyes grew large. He swallowed and his Adam's apple bobbed up and down. He rubbed his

forehead as though he had a headache.

Then Dink told Mr. Linkletter about Room 302. "Miss Nugent said there was a Do Not Disturb sign on the door."

Ruth Rose pointed to the register. "See? The signature is all smudged!"

"We think the kidnappers are hiding Wallis Wallace in that room!" Josh said.

At the word "kidnappers," Mr. Linkletter closed his eyes. He opened a drawer, took out a bottle of headache pills, and put one on his tongue.

"Just to be on the safe side, perhaps we should check both rooms, Mr. Linkletter," Mavis said quietly.

"It'll just take a minute," Dink said.

Mr. Linkletter let out a big sigh. "Very well, but this is most unusual. Things run very smoothly at the Shangrila."

They all got into the elevator. No one spoke. Dink watched Mr. Linkletter jiggling his bunch of keys. Mr. Linkletter kept his eyes on the little arrow telling them which floor they were on.

The elevator door opened on the third floor. Mr. Linkletter unlocked Room 303. "Most unusual," he muttered.

The room was empty and spotlessly clean. "Strange, very strange," Mr. Linkletter said.

They moved to Room 302, where a Do Not Disturb sign still hung on the doorknob.

Mr. Linkletter knocked. They all leaned toward the door.

"Listen, I hear a voice!" Josh said.

"What's it saying?" Ruth Rose asked.

Then they all heard it.

The voice was muffled, but it was definitely yelling, "HELP!"

Chapter 9

Mr. Linkletter unlocked the door and shoved it open.

A man with curly blond hair stared back at them. He was sitting in a chair with his feet tied in front of him. His arms were tied behind his back. A towel was wrapped around his mouth.

"Oh, my goodness!" Mr. Linkletter cried.

Everyone rushed into the room.

Dink ran behind the chair to untie the man's hands while Josh untied his

feet.

Mavis unwrapped the towel from around his face.

"Thank goodness you got here!" the man said. "I'm Wallis Wallace. Someone knocked on my door last night. A voice said he was from room service. When I opened the door, two men dragged me in here and tied me up."

He looked at Dink. "You're Dink Duncan! I recognize you from the picture you sent. How did you find me?"

"We followed your itinerary," Dink said. He showed Mr. Wallace the sheet of paper. "We got it from Mr. Paskey and used it as a trail. The trail led us to this room!"

"I'm so sorry I missed the book signing," Wallis Wallace said. "As you can see, I was a bit tied up."

He smiled. Then he rubbed his jaw. "My mouth is sore from that towel. I

can't believe I was kidnapped! And I can't wait to get back to my safe little cottage in Maine."

"Can you describe the two guys who kidnapped you?" Dink asked. "We should tell Officer Fallon so he can try to find them."

Wallis Wallace stared at Dink. "The two guys? Oh...well, um, I don't think I'll—"

"HEY!" Ruth Rose suddenly yelled.

Everyone looked at her.

"What's the matter?" asked Dink. "You look funny, Ruth Rose."

Ruth Rose was staring at the red scarf draped around Mavis's neck. She pointed at the man who'd been tied up. "You're not Wallis Wallace!"

Then she looked at Mavis Green. "*You* are," she said quietly.

Chapter
10

"Ruth Rose, what are you talking about?" Josh said.

Dink didn't know what to think, except that he was getting a headache.

"What makes you think *I'm* Wallis Wallace?" Mavis asked.

Ruth Rose walked over to Mavis. "May I borrow your scarf?" she said.

Ruth Rose held the scarf up so everyone could see it. "When I first saw this scarf, I thought these little black letters were M's," she said. "M for Mavis."

She looked at Mavis Green. "But they're not M's, are they?"

She turned the scarf completely upside down. "What do they look like now?"

Dink stepped closer. "They're little W's now!"

"Right. Double-U, double-U for *Wallis Wallace!*" Ruth Rose pointed at the man. "You just said you live in a little cottage. But Wallis Wallace lives in a big *castle* in Maine. It says so on the cover of *The Silent Swamp.*"

Ruth Rose pointed at Mavis's book bag. "Seeing your bag again made me remember something I thought of today. Josh read that your castle was called Moose Manor. There's a picture of a moose on the side of your bag."

Ruth Rose handed the scarf back to Mavis. "And we read that Wallis Wallace's favorite color is green. You like green ice cream, and you chose Mavis Green for your fake name."

Everyone was staring at Ruth Rose, except for the man they had untied. He started laughing.

"The cat's out of the bag now, sis," he said.

Then Mavis laughed and gave Ruth Rose a hug.

"Yes, Ruth Rose," Mavis said. "I really *am* Wallis Wallace." She put her hand on the man's shoulder. "And this is my brother, Walker Wallace. We've been planning my 'kidnapping' for weeks!"

Dink stared at Mavis, or whoever she was. "You mean Wallis Wallace is a woman?" he said.

"Yes, Dink, I'm a woman, and I'm definitely Wallis Wallace." She winked at him. "Honest!"

Mavis, the real Wallis Wallace, sat on the bed. She took off her glasses and

pulled the barrettes out of her hair. She shook her hair until it puffed out in a mass of wild curls.

"Thank goodness I can be myself now!" she said. "All day I've had to act like timid Mavis Green. I can't wait to get out of this fuddy-duddy dress and into my jeans again!"

She kicked off her shoes and wiggled her toes in the air. "Boy, does that feel good!"

Dink blinked and shook his head. Mavis Green was really Wallis Wallace? He couldn't believe it. "But why did you pretend to be kidnapped?" he asked.

The real Wallis Wallace grinned at the kids' surprised faces. "I owe you an explanation," she said.

"My new book is about a children's mystery writer who gets kidnapped. In my book, some children rescue the

writer. I wanted to find out how *real* kids might solve the mystery," she explained.

She smiled at Dink. "Then your letter came, inviting me to Green Lawn. That's what gave me the idea to fake my own kidnapping. I'd become Mavis Green and watch what happened."

"Oh, yeah!" Dink said. "In your let-

ter, you said you were doing some research in Connecticut."

She nodded. "Yes, and I mentioned the word 'kidnap' in the letter to get you thinking along those lines." She smiled at the three kids. "I thought I'd have to give you more clues, but you solved the mystery all by yourselves!"

Dink laughed. "You recognized me in

the bookstore from my picture," he said. "And you didn't send *me* a picture so I wouldn't recognize *you!*"

"Then my nutty sister dragged *me* into her plan," Walker Wallace said. "I should be home checking my lobster pots."

"While you were eating lunch, Walker and I ate ours up here," Wallis said. "Then, just before two o'clock, I tied him in the chair and ran downstairs to meet you out front as Mavis."

Wallis Wallace threw back her head and laughed. "Do you remember downstairs when Dink said there was something fishy on the third floor?"

She got up and stood next to her brother. "Well, I'm always teasing Walker about smelling fishy from handling his lobster bait. So when you said something was *fishy* in the hotel, I had to pretend to cough so you wouldn't

know I was really laughing!"

"Boy, did you have us fooled," Dink said.

Wallis Wallace grinned. "Mr. Paskey was in on it. I had to tell him the truth. As you saw this morning at the Book Nook, my little scheme made him very nervous. I've promised him I'll come back and do a real book signing soon. But I'll be in disguise, so be prepared for anything!"

Dink shook his head. "I was so disappointed because I couldn't meet my favorite author this morning," he said. "And I've been with you all day and didn't even know it!"

She looked at Dink. "I'm so sorry I tricked you. Will you forgive me?"

Dink blushed. "Sure."

"I have a question," Josh said. "Where did you really sleep last night?"

"Right here in Room 302. A few

weeks ago, I telephoned to reserve two rooms next to each other. Last night, I checked into Room 303 as Wallis Wallace, the man. Up in Room 303, I took off the hat and coat and sunglasses. Then I sneaked back down to the lobby wearing a blond wig. I checked in again, this time into Room 302."

"Did you smudge the signature?" Ruth Rose asked.

"Oh, you noticed that!" Wallis said. "I'm so used to signing my real name in books, I started to write *Wallis*. So I 'accidentally' smudged it."

"I have a question, Mavis, I mean Miss Wallace...what should we call you?" Dink asked.

"My friends call me Wallis," she said.

"Well, the taxi driver told us you were smiling in the taxi. What were you smiling about?"

Wallis Wallace was smiling now.

"Oh, about a lot of things. First, I was wearing a man's disguise, and that made me feel pretty silly. And I knew I was going to meet you, one of my biggest fans. And I was happy because I knew whatever happened, the next day would be fun!"

"I sure had fun," Josh said, grinning. "Poor Mr. Paskey, having to lie to everyone with a straight face!"

"Boy, did I have a hard time pretending to be Mavis all day," Wallis said. "But my plan worked. I met three brilliant detectives. You helped me to see how real kids would investigate a kidnapping. Now I can go back to Maine and finish my book."

"How come your book jackets never say that you're a woman?" Ruth Rose asked.

Wallis Wallace smiled. "Because of my name, most people assume that I'm a man," she explained. "I let them think that so I can do my research easier. I've learned that people clam up if they know I'm Wallis Wallace. So out in public I pretend I'm Mavis Green, just a regular person, not a mystery writer."

"I get it!" Dink said. "You don't have your picture on your books so people can't recognize you."

"Right. And I hope you'll keep my secret."

"We will. Right, guys?" Ruth Rose said.

"Thank you! Any more questions?" Wallis asked.

"Yeah," Walker said, giving his sister a look. "When do we leave? I've got lobsters waiting for me."

"I have a question, too," Dink said. "Will you send me your picture now?"

"Yes, but I'll do better than that," Wallis said. "I'll dedicate my next book

to my three new friends!"

Dink, Josh, and Ruth Rose did a triple high five.

"Excuse me," Mr. Linkletter said from the door where he had been standing.

They all looked at him.

"It's nearly checkout time."

Everyone laughed.

Mr. Linkletter smiled, but just a little.

This is the end of
The Absent Author

Collect clues with Dink, Josh, and Ruth Rose
in their next exciting adventure!
The Bald Bandit

Turn the page to start reading!

The
Bald
Bandit

by Ron Roy

illustrated by
John Steven Gurney

A STEPPING STONE BOOK™

Random House 🏠 New York

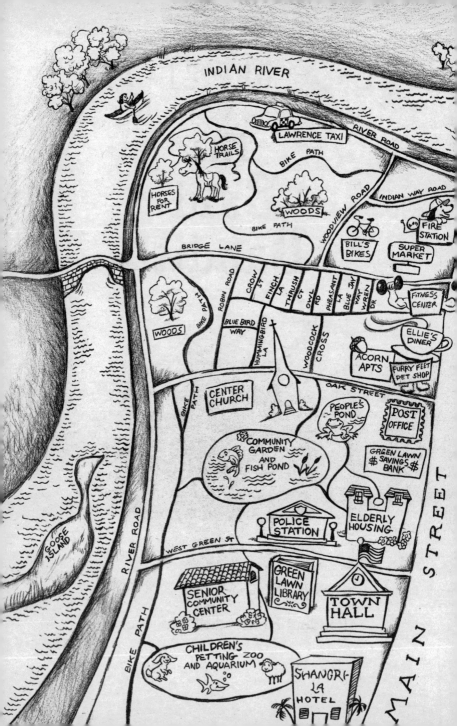

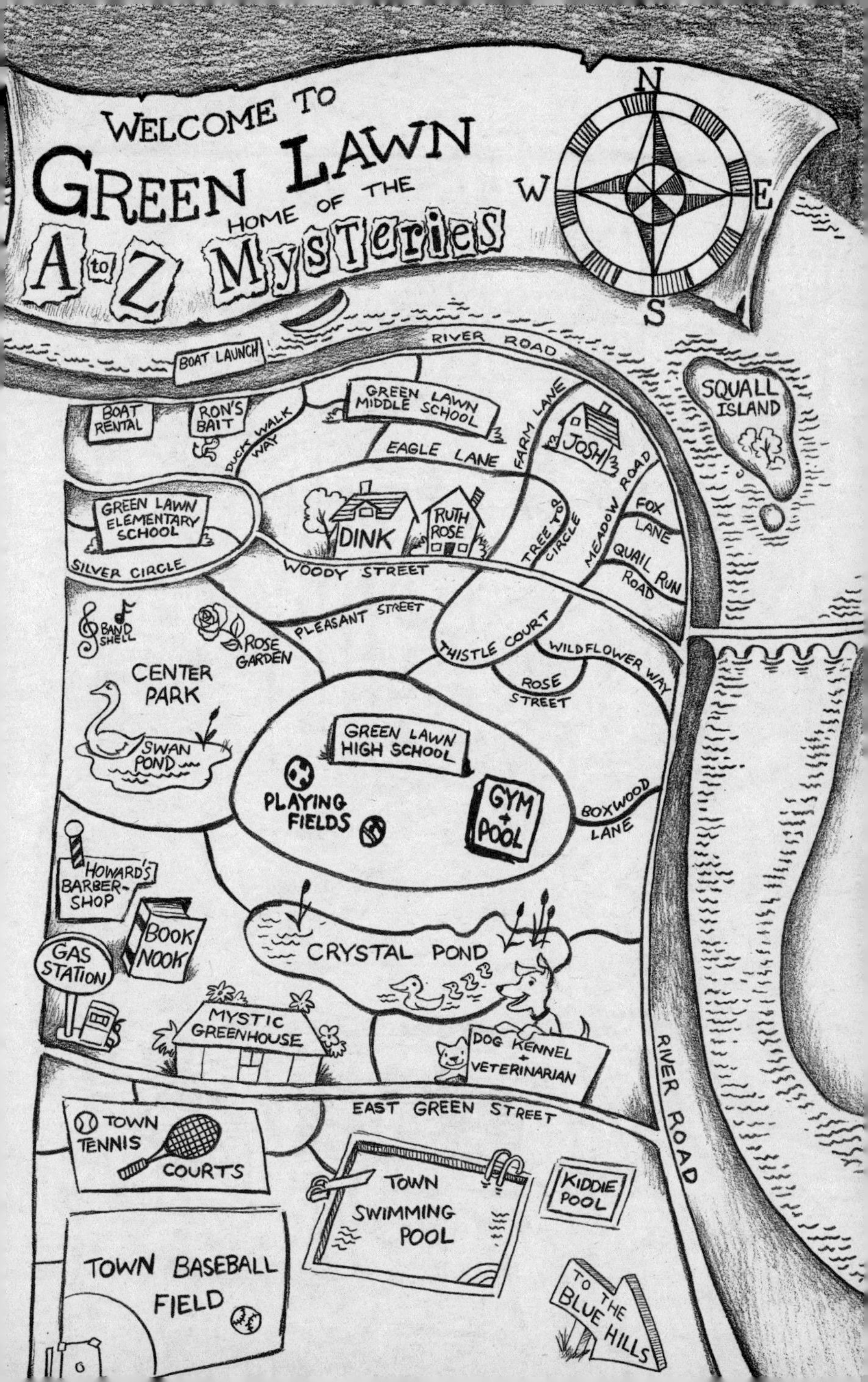

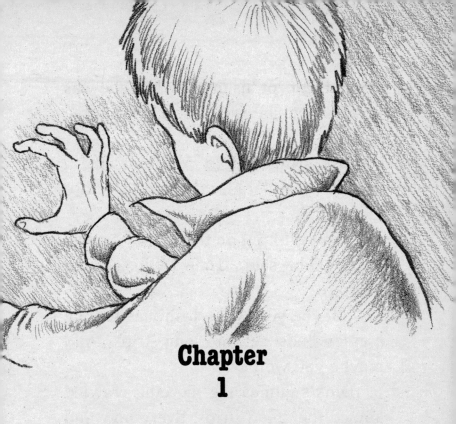

Chapter 1

Dink slipped the plastic fangs into his mouth. He made a scary face at his best friend, Josh Pinto.

"Do I look like a vampire?" It was hard to talk without spitting, so Dink took the fangs out again.

Dink's full name was Donald David Duncan, but nobody called him

Donald. Except his mom, when she was upset. Then she called him by all three names.

Josh grinned. "No. You look like a skinny third-grader wearing false teeth."

"Wait till I put on the rest of my costume," Dink said. "Then I'll look like a vampire."

"Maybe you will." Josh was tearing a green bedsheet into long strips. "And maybe you won't."

Dink's guinea pig, Loretta, crawled among the green strips. Every now and then she let out a curious squeak.

"How will you be able to walk if you're wrapped up in all those strips?" Dink asked Josh.

Josh kept tearing. "Swamp monsters don't walk," he said in a slithery voice. "They *gliiiide.*"

"Okay, so how will you be able to

gliiiide wrapped up in all those strips?"

The doorbell rang. When Dink opened the door, his next-door neighbor, Ruth Rose, was standing on the steps.

"Hi, Ruth Rose. Why are you wearing a wig? Halloween isn't until tomorrow."

Ruth Rose was dressed in her usual bright clothes—a pink shirt, pink pants, and pink sneakers. But on her head she wore a shiny black wig. She also had on thick fake eyebrows.

Ruth Rose wiggled the fake eyebrows up and down. "Guess who I am!"

Josh stared at Ruth Rose. "A hairy princess?"

"No."

"Groucho Marx?"

She shook her head.

"Tell us, Ruth Rose," Dink said.

Ruth Rose pretended to strum a

guitar. "I'm Elvis!" she cried.

"That was my next guess," Josh said.

Ruth Rose looked at his mound of green strips. "What are you supposed to be?"

Josh wrapped a strip around his face. He made a swamp monster face at Ruth Rose.

"Guess," he said.

Ruth Rose smiled sweetly. "You're a green sheet torn into strips."

The doorbell rang again.

This time Dink saw a tall man standing on the doorstep. He was dressed in a suit and tie. He had dark curly hair, a droopy mustache, and a dimpled chin.

"Hi, there. My name is Detective Reddy. I was hired by the Green Lawn Savings Bank to find someone. Did you hear about the robbery?"

Josh and Ruth Rose came to the

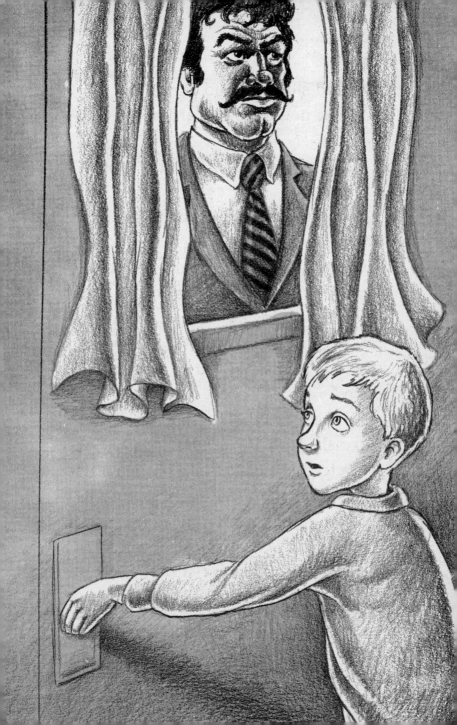

door and stood behind Dink.

Dink nodded. "I heard about it on TV."

"Are you looking for the robber?" Josh asked.

Detective Reddy shook his head. "Right now I'm looking for someone who saw him. When the thief ran out of the bank, he took off his mask. Some kid was walking by with a video camera. He got the thief on tape. The bank hired me to find the kid so I can get the video."

"What does the kid look like?" Ruth Rose asked.

Detective Reddy stared at her Elvis wig. "Someone in the bank said he has red hair and he's tall and skinny."

"Sounds like you, Josh," said Dink. He laughed and pointed at Josh's red hair.

"It wasn't me, honest!" Josh said. "I

don't even have a video camera."

"No, the kid was a lot older than you," said the detective. "Probably in high school." He patted his mustache. "Do you guys know anyone like that?"

"No," Dink said. "But we do know Green Lawn pretty well. Maybe we can help you find him."

The detective looked at the three friends.

"Tell you what," he said. "Check the high school tomorrow. If you find the kid who filmed the robber, get the video. There'll be a nice reward if you hand it over."

"How much?" Josh asked.

"How about one hundred dollars for each of you?"

"A HUNDRED BUCKS?" screamed Ruth Rose.

Dink, Josh, and Detective Reddy covered their ears.

"Ouch!" said Detective Reddy. "That's quite a set of lungs you've got there."

"How can we get in touch with you if we find the kid?" Dink asked.

The detective pulled out a small pad and a pencil. He wrote something and ripped off the page.

"Here's my phone number. Call me if you get that video."

Dink closed the door behind Detective Reddy. He grinned at Josh and Ruth Rose. "A hundred bucks each! We're rich!"

Chapter 2

"Here's the plan," Dink said.

It was almost three o'clock the next afternoon. Dink, Josh, and Ruth Rose were headed for the high school, a few blocks away from Green Lawn Elementary.

"Josh, you cover the back door. Ruth Rose, your station is the bike rack. But keep an eye on the parking lot, too."

"How can I watch the bike rack *and* the parking lot?" asked Ruth Rose.

"Watch one with each eye," Josh said, grinning.

"What's your station?" Ruth Rose asked Dink.

"I'll be watching the front door. If anyone sees a skinny redhead, stop him and yell."

Ruth Rose laughed. "Stop him and yell? He'll think we're crazy and run away."

"She's right," Josh said.

Dink scratched his thick blond hair. "Hmm. Okay, don't yell. Just get his name and tell him he may have won some money."

They cut through the park next to the high school.

"What money?" Josh asked.

"Well, if Detective Reddy is going to pay us a hundred dollars each to find the video, I figure we can give the kid half the money. But only if he gives us the video."

At the high school, they split up.

Josh ran around to the back of the
school. Ruth Rose sat on the lawn next
to the bike rack.

Dink sat on a bench where he had a
good view of the front door.

Suddenly, he heard a loud bell. Ten
seconds later, the front door burst open.
A million high school kids shoved

through the door and scrambled down the front steps.

Dink stood on the bench so he wouldn't get trampled. He was looking for red hair, but it wasn't easy to spot. Some of the kids had hats on. Some wore jackets or sweatshirts with the hoods pulled up. Sometimes Dink couldn't tell if a kid was a boy or a girl!

Finally, he spotted a tall guy with red hair. Dink jumped off the bench and ran after him.

"Excuse me," Dink said, trying to catch his breath.

"Who are you?" the redhead asked.

"Dink Duncan." Dink tried to remember his plan. "You may have won some money!"

The redhead stared down at Dink. "Money? Me? Why? How much money?"

"Were you near the bank when the

robbery happened last week?" he asked.

The kid kept staring at Dink. "Robbery? What robbery?"

"You didn't hear about it? It was on the news, on TV. Some guy robbed Green Lawn Savings Bank."

"So what's it to you?"

"A kid with red hair got the robber on tape," Dink said. "I'm helping to find him. There's going to be a reward."

"Rats, I wish I did tape the guy," the redhead said, shaking his head. "I could use a reward. But I wasn't anywhere near the bank last week." He waved and headed for the park. "Good luck!"

Dink looked around for another redhead, but everyone had disappeared.

He walked toward the bike rack. Ruth Rose was sitting on the lawn, weaving grass blades together.

"Did you see any redheads?" Dink

asked, plopping down beside her.

"Three," Ruth Rose said. "One was a short, fat boy. One was a girl. One was a teacher."

Josh came running up.

"Any luck?" he asked.

"Nope," Dink said. "How'd you do?"

"I talked to two guys with red hair. One of them told me to take a hike. The other one was an exchange student from Ireland. He told me he doesn't even know where the bank is."

"Great," Dink said. "We all struck out. Now what do we do?"

Josh tossed a pine cone at a tree. "Beats me."

"We should search the whole neighborhood," Ruth Rose said.

"How?" Dink asked.

Ruth Rose stood up and dusted off her shorts. "Easy. We just go door to door and ask."

"How can we do that without our parents finding out?" Josh asked. "Mine won't let me get involved with some bank robber, that's for sure."

"Mine either," Dink said.

"So how do we explain why we're wandering around Green Lawn knocking on everyone's doors?" asked Josh.

"Come on, guys," Ruth Rose said. "Think about it. What's tonight?"

Dink and Josh looked at each other.

"Halloween!"

Chapter 3

With black shoe polish in his hair and plastic fangs in his mouth, Dink looked like Dracula.

His mom had made him a cape from an old black raincoat. He tied the cape around his neck just as the doorbell rang.

A strange creature stood on his porch. The thing was wrapped in green cloth. Tufts of red hair poked out at the top. Large black high-tops stuck out at the bottom.

"How do I look?" the thing asked.

Dink took out his fangs and grinned. "Like some weird vegetable. Half carrot and half asparagus."

Josh shuffled inside the house.

"You look pretty good, Dink. I like the blood dripping down your chin."

The bell dinged again. This time it was a miniature Elvis. Ruth Rose was wearing a white suit with sequins everywhere. She even carried a little guitar. Her Elvis wig made her look about two inches taller.

Ruth Rose strummed her guitar and wiggled her hips.

"Thank you very much, ladies and gentlemen," she said, taking a bow.

"Come on in, Elvis," Dink said. "We have to talk about Operation Redhead before we go trick-or-treating."

They sat at Dink's kitchen table. A basket of candy stood waiting for the neighborhood kids.

"Here's my plan," Dink said. "Every house we go to, we ask if anyone knows a skinny redheaded kid."

"That's *my* plan!" Ruth Rose said.

Dink grinned. "Oh, yeah, I forgot."

One of Ruth Rose's black eyebrows was crooked. "We have to keep our eyes peeled. Check out tall kids trick-or-treating."

"Got it," Dink said.

"Anyone with red hair, we ask them if they took a video of the bank robber," Ruth Rose went on.

"Check," Dink said. "Any other ideas?"

"Yeah, I got a great idea," Josh said. "Let's stop talking and get moving!"

Dink's mother walked into the kitchen. She screamed and clutched her chest.

"Oh, my goodness! Monsters in my kitchen!"

Ruth Rose stood up. "I'm not a monster, Mrs. Duncan. I'm Elvis!"

Dink's mom adjusted Ruth Rose's left eyebrow. "I know, honey. You make a great Elvis. But these other two!" She shuddered and made a terrified face.

"We're going now, Mom." Dink fit the plastic fangs over his teeth. He handed Josh a paper bag and took one for himself.

"Please be back in two hours," his mother said. "Dad and I will have some cider and doughnuts for you."

The three kids each took a different street. They agreed to meet back at Dink's house in about two hours.

Dink headed down Woody Street. He looked at every tall kid in a costume, checking for red hair. But most of the kids out were shorter than him. He counted seventeen ghosts, twenty little witches, eight angels with floppy wings, and a zillion small furry animals.

Dink rang Mrs. Davis's doorbell. "Trick or treat!"

"Oh, hello, Dink!" said Mrs. Davis. She dropped a small bag of candy kisses into his sack.

"Have you seen any redheaded kids tonight?" Dink asked.

"Redheads?" Mrs. Davis patted her white hair. "I'm afraid I don't know anyone besides your friend Josh who has red hair."

Dink thanked Mrs. Davis for the candy and walked next door to old Mr. Kramer's house.

Mr. Kramer was a little deaf.

"Do you know a skinny redhead?" asked Dink in a loud voice.

Mr. Kramer turned one ear and leaned toward Dink. "What's that you say? A tinny red bed?"

"A skinny red*head!*" Dink yelled
even louder. He wished he had Ruth
Rose with him. She was the only one
loud enough for Mr. Kramer to hear.

Mr. Kramer dropped a nickel in
Dink's bag and slammed the door. Dink
sighed.

He followed some ghosts to the next
house on Woody Street.

A gorilla opened the door when
Dink rang the bell. It had a hairy chest
and a huge mouth filled with yellow
teeth.

"Trick or treat!" said Dink.

The gorilla dropped a banana into
Dink's bag.

"Have you seen any tall redheaded
teenagers walking around?" Dink
asked.

The gorilla grunted and shook his
head.

"Thanks anyway," said Dink.

Two hours later, Dink, Josh, and Ruth Rose poured their candy onto Dink's dining room table.

Dink took out his fangs. "Any luck?" he asked.

Josh unwrapped his face. "I saw four redheads. Two girls about ten years old and two adults. No one I talked to knew a skinny redhead in high school."

Ruth Rose took off her wig and eyebrows and dropped them into her plastic jack-o'-lantern.

"Same here," she sighed, slumping in her chair. "Nobody knew the right redhead. And I asked everybody!"

Josh ripped open a miniature bag of M&M's.

"I really wanted that hundred bucks," he said. "Maybe we should just forget it."

"Give up after just two days? No way, you guys!" Dink climbed up on the table. He wrapped his cape around his face so just his eyes showed.

In his best Count Dracula voice, he said, *"Vee vill never giff up!"*

Chapter 4

The next morning, Dink's hair was stiff with black shoe polish. He shampooed three times before he got out of the shower.

The bathroom mirror was fogged up when he tried to see his reflection. He wiped the mirror, looked at himself, and gasped.

His hair wasn't its usual blond and it wasn't vampire black. It was a muddy brown color, like the rusty parts on his bike.

"Mom! Help!"

His mother peeked into the bathroom. "What's the...oh, I see." She giggled.

"It's not funny, Mom. How am I supposed to go outside like this? My hair looks like it rusted!"

"Honey, lots of kids will have traces of makeup on their faces or color in their hair today. It's the day after Halloween."

Dink rubbed a towel over his hair as hard as he could. He looked in the mirror. Now he had *frizzy* rust-colored hair.

"Be thankful it's Saturday," his mother said, smiling. "At least you don't have to go to school today."

After breakfast, Dink jammed his baseball cap over his hair and headed for Josh's house.

When Dink got there, Josh was already shooting hoops in front of his barn. He grinned at Dink.

"What's wrong with your hair?" he asked.

Dink yanked his hat off. "Take a look. The stupid shoe polish from last night won't wash out. I had to be a vampire, right? I couldn't just be a cowboy or an astronaut."

Josh dribbled and took a shot. He missed the hoop.

"So have you thought of a plan for finding that kid with the video?" Josh asked.

"No," said Dink, jamming his hat back over his hair.

"Well, what do we do now?" said Josh. "Ask at more houses?"

"I don't know," Dink said. "Now that Halloween is over, we'd look pretty suspicious. Besides, Green Lawn has hundreds of houses. We'd be knocking on doors for a month."

Josh made a perfect shot. "Two points!"

"We have to use our heads instead of our feet," Dink said, grabbing the ball after Josh's basket.

A door slammed behind them.

"Uh-oh," Josh mumbled.

"Josh, it's time to go," his mother called. "Come in and brush your teeth, please."

"I have a dentist appointment," Josh said. "Call me later, okay?"

"Okay." Dink tossed Josh's ball into the barn and started walking away.

"Hey!" Josh yelled behind him. "I think your new hair color looks just *adorable!*"

"Very funny," Dink muttered, tugging his hat down even tighter.

Maybe I'll cut my hair off, he thought. *Go to school bald on Monday.*

Suddenly, he stopped walking.

Thinking about cutting his hair off gave him an idea.

He ran toward Main Street. At Howard's Barbershop, he peered through the glass. Howard was watching an *I Love Lucy* rerun on a small TV set.

Dink walked in, setting off the sleigh bells hanging over the door. Whenever he came to Howard's for a haircut, Dink thought about Christmas.

"What'll it be today, Dink?" Howard asked. "Want a flattop? How about one of them Mohawk jobbies, with the stripe down the middle?"

"I don't want a haircut," Dink said. "I need to ask you something."

Howard squinted one blue eye. He lifted Dink's baseball cap. "What happened to your hair?"

Dink blushed. "I was a vampire last night. I used black shoe polish in my

hair and it won't come out. I tried."

Howard grinned. "Hop up in the chair, me lad. I'll dose you with me special shampoo. You can ask your question while I perform a little magic."

Dink hung his hat on a peg and

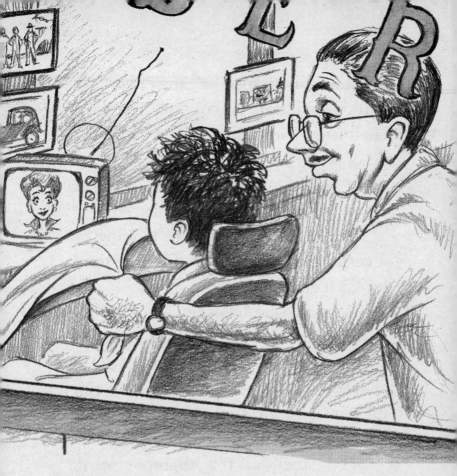

climbed into the barber chair. Howard
pulled a bottle and some white towels
out of a cupboard.

"I was wondering if you know any
kids with red hair," Dink said. "Besides
Josh."

Howard draped a towel around Dink's shoulders and pinned it in back. He misted Dink's hair with a spray bottle of water.

"I might," he answered. "Why, do you want me to dye your hair red?"

Dink laughed. "No, I'm looking for a certain kid who has red hair. I think he's a teenager."

"I know one teenager who *had* red hair," Howard said, pouring green shampoo onto Dink's hair. "But I shaved it all off last week. Came running in here all excited, out of breath. 'Shave my head!' he tells me. So I did."

The smell of the shampoo made Dink's eyes water. He felt his heart start to tap-dance.

"Was he carrying a video camera?" Dink asked.

Howard rubbed the shampoo into Dink's hair.

"Why all the questions about this redheaded boy?" he asked.

Dink thought for a few seconds, then decided to spill the beans. He told Howard about the bank robber, about the kid with the video camera, and about the three hundred dollars the detective had promised.

Howard chuckled. "Oh, now I see why the boy ran in here yelling for me to cut off all his hair. He didn't want the bank bandit to recognize him. So if I tell you this lad's name, you're going to persuade him to give you the videotape?"

"Yes, if I can," Dink said.

"What about the money?" said Howard.

Dink looked at Howard in the mirror. "What about it?"

"Would you be planning to share the reward with the redheaded boy?"

Dink grinned. "Sure. We'll give him

half of what we get from the detective."

"That sounds like a fine idea." Howard rubbed Dink's hair vigorously. Dink watched in the mirror. His hair was a slimy green mess.

"Does this stuff really get shoe polish out?" he asked.

"Yup. Invented it meself," Howard said. "Secret recipe. I used it once to get bubble gum out of me granddaughter's hair. It took tar out of our dog's fur, too."

Howard swung the barber chair around and lowered its back. He positioned Dink's head over the sink.

"Close your eyes, me boy. Let's wash this gook out and see what's what."

Dink liked the feel of the warm water and Howard's fingers smoothing the shampoo out of his hair. After a few minutes, Howard sat him up and plopped a fresh towel on his head.

"Dry off. I think you're back to normal."

Dink rubbed his hair with the towel, then looked in the mirror. He laughed out loud. "You did it!"

Howard smiled at Dink's reflection. "I should sell this stuff and make a million dollars."

"How much do I owe you?" Dink asked.

"This one's on me, young fella. And the boy with red hair is Lucky O'Leary. He lives over on Robin Road with his mum and his little brothers and sisters. All six of 'em! Nice kids, and every last one's a redhead."

Howard grinned as he lowered the chair.

"Except for Lucky, who suddenly decided to go bald."

Chapter 5

"He's *bald?*" Josh said, climbing Ruth Rose's front steps.

Dink had run right home from the barbershop and called Josh. Now they were picking up Ruth Rose so they could go to Robin Road together.

"That's what Howard said," Dink told Josh. He pushed the doorbell.

"So that's why we didn't spot him at the high school!" Josh said.

"COME IN!" Ruth Rose screamed from inside.

Ruth Rose was sitting on the floor

watching a video with her four-year-old brother, Nate.

"Come on, Ruth Rose. I think we found the redhead!" Dink said. "We're going to his house."

Ruth Rose jumped up and screamed, "I'M LEAVING WITH THE GUYS, MOM! WATCH NATE!"

Dink and Josh covered their ears.

Ruth Rose told Nate, "You stay right here and wait for Mommy, okay?"

Nate nodded and kept his eyes on the TV set.

"Let's go." Ruth Rose led the way back to the door and skipped down the front steps.

"How'd you find the kid?" she asked.

Dink explained how he hadn't been able to get the shoe polish out of his hair.

"That made me think about cutting

my hair off. And *that* made me think about the barbershop. Who would know all the redheads in Green Lawn?"

"HOWARD THE BARBER!" she screamed.

The boys covered their ears again.

"I'm going to need a hearing aid like old Mr. Kramer," Josh muttered.

Dink had looked up O'Leary in the phone book to get the address on Robin Road. They stopped in front of house number 33. It was a big blue house with toys and bikes and sneakers and basketballs all over the lawn. Loud music came out through the front door.

They walked onto the porch and stepped over a baseball bat. Four pumpkins sat in a row, all carved with scary faces.

Dink rang the bell. "Keep your fingers crossed," he said.

A little girl opened the door. She

had red hair and a face full of freckles.

"Hi! I'm Josephine and I'm five and a half!" She held up ten fingers.

"Is your brother home?" Dink asked.

"Which one? I have this many!" Josephine held up ten fingers again.

Dink laughed. "Do you have a big brother named Lucky?"

The music went off.

"Who's out there, Jo?" a voice called. A tall, skinny teenager wearing torn jeans and a T-shirt came up behind Josephine. Dink noticed red fuzz covering his head, like a new red lawn.

"Are you Lucky O'Leary?" Dink asked.

The kid looked down at Dink and Josh and Ruth Rose. "Who wants to know?"

"We do," Ruth Rose said. "How'd you like to earn some money?"

"I might," he said.

"We're looking for a kid who got the Green Lawn bank robber on video last week," Dink said. "The bank hired a detective to find the video, and we're helping the detective. He's paying us to get the video, and we'll split the money with you. If you're the kid, I mean."

"Are you?" Ruth Rose asked.

The kid rubbed the top of his fuzzy red head. "Yeah," he muttered. "I'm the guy."

Then he crossed his arms. "But I'm not giving my tape to any detective."

Chapter 6

The kids stared at Lucky.

"Why not?" Ruth Rose asked. "The detective is helping the bank find the robber. You could be a HERO!"

"Shh!" said Lucky. He looked around nervously. Then he beckoned Dink, Josh, and Ruth Rose inside.

"Come on."

Inside Lucky's house, the kids followed him down a hallway into his bedroom. Dink noticed that he was limping. His room had posters of basketball players on the walls. There were clothes all over the floor.

Lucky flopped down on his bed.

"Listen," he said. "I'm afraid to give that tape to the detective. What if the robber found out I handed it over? With my luck, he'd come after me."

"How would the robber know it was you who taped him?" Dink asked.

Lucky sat up. "Because he looked right at me when he ran out of the bank. The guy saw me taping him! That's why I ran to Howard's to get my head shaved." Lucky scratched his fuzzy head.

"But if you turn in the tape, the robber will get caught. Then you won't have to worry about him at all," said Josh.

"Besides, we'll give you half of our reward," Ruth Rose said. "Right, guys?"

"Right," Dink said. "Is Lucky your real name?"

The kid shook his head. "It's Paul. Lucky is my nickname. People call me that because I always have such rotten luck. Since school started, my dog died, my bike got stolen, and I broke my toe. I can barely walk to school."

"You can buy a new bike with the reward money," Ruth Rose said. "Then you won't have to walk."

Lucky smiled at Ruth Rose. "I'm saving all my money for college," he said. Then he sighed. "It seems like I'll never get enough."

Lucky thought for a minute.

"Listen, that reward money would really help," he said. "But you guys have to *promise* not to tell who gave you the video."

They all nodded.

"Okay," said Lucky. He got off the bed and limped over to his closet. He pulled a box from the top shelf. The box

was filled with videotapes. He handed
one of the tapes to Dink.

Lucky looked embarrassed. "Um...

when can I get the money?" he asked.

"Maybe tomorrow," Dink said. "We'll let you know, okay?"

"Sure, that'll be fine," said Lucky. He pretended to zip his lips closed. "And remember, you promised not to tell anyone where you got the video. Not even that detective."

The kids nodded again.

Lucky walked them to the door, stepping around a pile of kids wrestling on the living room floor. Dink noticed they all had red hair and freckles.

Josephine popped up out of the pile. "Bye!" she said, smiling at Dink.

As soon as they were on the sidewalk, Dink, Josh, and Ruth Rose triple-high-fived each other.

"We got it!" Josh yelled.

Dink slipped the tape into his pocket. "Now we just have to call Detective Reddy and get our money!"

Chapter 7

The kids hurried back to Dink's house. There was no one home. Dink opened the front door with his key.

He saw a note on the kitchen table.

DAD AND I ARE OUT SHOPPING. WE'LL BE BACK SOON. HAVE A SNACK. LOVE, MOM

Dink was glad his folks were out. He knew they wouldn't like him playing detective. When this was all over, he'd tell them how he earned the hundred bucks.

Josh opened Dink's refrigerator. "What do you have to eat?" he asked.

Dink set the tape on the counter. "There should be some doughnuts on the counter."

He pulled the paper with the detective's number on it out of his pocket. He called the number.

"Hello, is this Detective Reddy? This is Dink Duncan. Me and my friends found that video for you. What? No, we haven't looked at it. Okay. Bye."

Dink hung up smiling. "He'll be right over. He said we were good detectives. He told us not to look at the video."

Josh was eating a doughnut. "Why

not?" he said with his mouth full.

"He said it was top secret."

They all looked at each other.

"Come on!" Dink said, grabbing the video.

They ran into the living room. Dink turned on the TV and slid the tape into the VCR.

The first part of the video showed a big dog chewing on a rubber bone. Then they saw a girl in a bathing suit. She was laughing and running away from the camera. Next came a birthday party. Most of the people in the picture looked like Lucky O'Leary. Dink recognized little Josephine.

Finally, they saw the front of the Green Lawn Savings Bank. The door opened and a man came running out. He was pulling off a ski mask.

"That must be the robber!" Dink said. He pressed the pause button.

The man on the tape was completely bald. His head was shiny in the sunlight. He was wearing sweatpants and a sweatshirt, and he was carrying a gym bag. He had a surprised look on his face.

"That must be when he noticed Lucky taping him," Josh said.

Ruth Rose moved closer to the TV. "Look, he's got a dimple on his chin."

Suddenly, Ruth Rose gasped. She ran across the room and out of the house. The door slammed behind her.

Dink looked at Josh. "What's going on?"

Josh shrugged. "Maybe she doesn't like guys with dimples."

A minute later, the door burst open and Ruth Rose ran back in. She was carrying her Elvis wig and her fake eyebrows.

Ruth Rose stuck one eyebrow on the

TV screen, under the bandit's nose. It looked like a mustache. She held the wig over the bandit's bald head.

"Who does that look like?" she demanded.

Josh jumped into the air. "Oh, my gosh! The bank robber looks exactly

like Detective Reddy!"

Just then the doorbell rang. Dink peeked through the front window.

"Who is it?" Josh asked.

Dink's eyes were bugging out when he turned around. "It's Detective Reddy!"

Chapter 8

Ruth Rose snatched the wig and eyebrow off the TV and hid them behind
her back.

Josh pushed the eject button and
slid the video inside his shirt.

Dink stared at the door. He didn't
think he could walk.

The bell rang again.

Dink looked at his friends. Then he
took a deep breath and opened the
door.

Ruth Rose slipped out just as
Detective Reddy walked in.

"Hi, there," said Detective Reddy. He grinned at Dink and Josh. "Gee, you kids are clever. How'd you find the redhead with the video?"

Dink stared at the man in front of him. He couldn't believe it. Detective Reddy wasn't a detective at all. He was a bank robber! And he was standing in Dink's own living room!

"We were just lucky, I guess," Dink mumbled.

The man patted his mustache. "So where is it?"

Dink wouldn't let his eyes look at the lump under Josh's shirt. "Where's what?"

"The video. You called and said you had the video. So where is it?"

Dink's mind went blank. He didn't know what to say.

Think, Dink! he commanded himself.

Josh came to the rescue. "We hid the tape upstairs, remember, Dink?"

Dink stared at Josh. "Huh? Oh, yeah, now I remember." He grinned at the man. "We wanted to make sure no one saw it before we gave it to you."

"Come on, Dink." Josh headed for the stairs.

"It takes two of you to get one video?" the man said.

"Well...um...it's in my mother's room." Dink held up his front door key. "I'm the only one allowed to unlock her door."

Dink hurried up the stairs behind Josh. They ran into Dink's bedroom and shut the door.

Dink's guinea pig, Loretta, started squeaking and running around in her cage.

"Not now, Loretta," Dink said.

"Where'd Ruth Rose go?" said Josh.

"I can't believe she ditched us!"

Dink didn't answer. He paced back and forth in front of his bed. He tugged on his hair. He snapped his fingers nervously.

"Dink, stop, I'm getting dizzy," Josh said. "What're we gonna do?"

Dink stopped. "I don't know! We can't give him the video. He'll destroy it. Then nobody can prove anything! He'll get away scot-free. And he might even go after Lucky!"

"We have to catch him and hand him over to the cops," Josh said. "Do you have any rope? We'll jump him and tie him up!"

"I don't keep rope in my bedroom, Josh," Dink said. "Besides, he's bigger and stronger than us. He might even have a gun!"

"Need any help up there?" the man yelled.

Dink opened his door a crack. "No thanks. We'll be right down."

Dink grabbed a soccer video from his bookshelf and handed it to Josh. "Let's give him this."

"But what happens when he finds

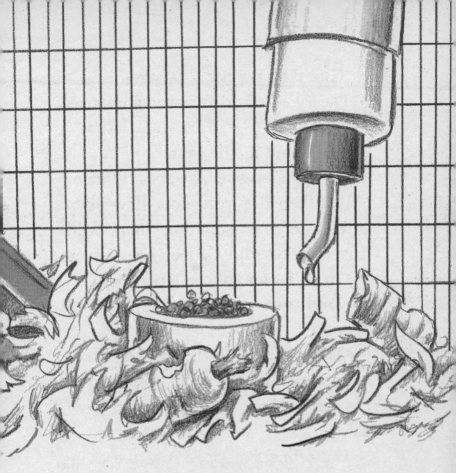

out it's not the real video?" Josh asked.

"I don't know. But we don't have any choice."

Josh pulled Lucky's video out of his shirt. He dropped it in Loretta's cage and covered it with shavings.

"Guard it, Loretta," he said.

They walked downstairs. Dink tried to smile.

"We found it!" he said.

Josh handed over the soccer video.

Just then the front door flew open. Ruth Rose was standing there with Officer Fallon and Officer Keene from the Green Lawn Police Department.

Dink was never so happy to see anyone.

"That's him!" Ruth Rose declared. She pointed at the man holding the videotape. "He robbed the Green Lawn bank!"

The officers stepped into the living room.

The man smiled. "I'm a private detective, officers," he said.

"Mind showing us some identification, sir?" said Officer Fallon.

The man patted his mustache. "I

don't have my wallet with me."

"You don't?" Officer Keene said. "Detectives are required to carry their identification at all times."

"Sure, and normally I do. But I left my wallet in the car. I'll get it and be right back."

"His mustache is fake!" Ruth Rose said, stepping in front of the officers. "And so is that wig!"

Everybody stared at the man.

Suddenly, he grabbed Ruth Rose and held her in front of him.

"Outta my way!" he yelled. "I'm leaving, and the girl's coming with me!"

Ruth Rose took a deep breath.

Then she let out the loudest scream of her life.

"AIIIIIIIIIEEEEEEEEE!"

Chapter
9

Josh, Dink, and the officers covered their ears.

"Ouch!" cried the bank robber.

He stumbled backward, clapping his hands over his ears.

The minute he let go of Ruth Rose, Officer Fallon grabbed him.

"It's all over, fella," Officer Fallon said. He snapped handcuffs on the man's wrists.

Officer Keene pulled off the thief's fake mustache and wig. Now the man looked just the way he did in the video. He had a shiny bald head and a surprised look on his face.

Officer Keene took him outside.

Officer Fallon put his hand on Ruth Rose's shoulder. "Ruth Rose, are you all right?"

Ruth Rose nodded. "I'm fine, Officer Fallon."

"So where's this videotape you told me about?"

Josh ran upstairs and got Lucky's video. He came back and slid it into the VCR. While they watched, Dink told Officer Fallon how it all happened.

Officer Fallon laughed. "Pretty clever of our thief. He hired you to find the video with his own face in it. If he got rid of the tape, no one could prove he was in that bank."

"He couldn't look for the tape himself," Ruth Rose explained. "The kid who taped him might have recognized him, like I did."

"How did you kids get hold of this video?" Officer Fallon asked.

Dink remembered their promise to Lucky. "We can't tell where we got it. We promised."

Officer Fallon smiled. "Well, whoever caught that guy on tape deserves a reward. Speaking of which, I believe you kids will be sharing a five-thousand-dollar reward from the bank."

"Five thousand dollars!" Josh jumped out of his seat. He and Dink did a little dance around the living room.

Officer Fallon laughed. "Ruth Rose here is a brave girl. She snuck over to her house and called the police station."

Ruth Rose turned her favorite shade of pink.

When Officer Fallon left, Ruth Rose did some math on Dink's calculator. "After we give Lucky his half, we'll each get $833.33," she said. "With a penny left over."

"We're rich!" said Josh. "Let's spend it!"

Dink laughed. "Mine's going into my savings account."

"Mine, too," Ruth Rose said. "I'm saving for a computer."

Josh slumped into a chair. "Yeah, you're right. My folks would kill me if I blew eight hundred bucks on pizza and ice cream."

On Monday, Dink, Josh, and Ruth Rose ran to the high school as soon as Green Lawn Elementary let out. They sat on a bench in front of the high school, out of breath.

"What did Lucky say when you told him he's getting half of five thousand dollars?" Josh asked.

"Nothing," Dink said, smiling. "I didn't tell him."

Just then the bell rang. A few seconds later, kids came streaming out of the high school.

"There he is!" Ruth Rose ran to meet Lucky O'Leary. She brought him over to the bench. He was smiling.

"Ruth Rose says you got paid. Did you bring my hundred and fifty?" he asked.

Dink shook his head sadly. "Not exactly."

"What do you mean, 'Not exactly'?"

The three friends burst out laughing.

"We don't have a hundred and fifty

dollars, but we do have this," said Dink.

He handed Lucky a check for $2,500.

Lucky's mouth and eyes popped open. "Twenty-five hundred bucks!" he yelled. "Where did *this* come from?"

"That's your half of the reward from the bank," Dink said. "We looked at your tape when we got home. Ruth Rose recognized the robber. He turned out to be the detective, only he wasn't really a detective. He was just pretending to be one so he could find you to get your video."

Lucky blinked. "So you guys nabbed him?"

"Yeah, right in Dink's house!" Josh said. "Ruth Rose snuck out and called the cops."

"It was exciting!" said Ruth Rose.

Lucky stared at his check again. He shook his head and grinned. "This is my lucky day. Now my mom can get the kids all their school stuff and have the car fixed."

"What about college?" Dink asked. "I thought that's what you were going to do with your money."

Lucky shook his head. "College is out for now. I'll have to work for a while till Mom and I can save more." Lucky looked at his check. "Maybe next year."

He shook hands with the three kids. "Anyway, thanks a lot for this check. I can't wait to see my mom's face when I give it to her!"

Dink watched Lucky walk away. Only he wasn't limping as much today.

"I wonder how many college courses Lucky could buy with my $833.33," he said.

Ruth Rose smiled at Dink. "I wonder how many college books he could buy with mine," she said.

Josh stared. "What? You're giving *your* money to Lucky? But you earned it!"

Dink shook his head. "No, we didn't. We just ran around talking to people. Lucky really earned the reward money."

"That's right," Ruth Rose said. "He's the one who caught the robber on videotape."

Dink and Ruth Rose started walking toward Main Street.

"Hey, where you guys going?" Josh yelled.

"To the bank," Dink said over his shoulder. "And then to Lucky's house."

Ruth Rose turned around and looked at Josh. "You coming with us?"

Josh grinned, then caught up with Dink and Ruth Rose. "I wonder how many college *meals* Lucky can buy with my $833.33," he said.

"Race you to the bank!" said Ruth
Rose.

And the three friends took off.

This is the end of

The Bald Bandit

Collect clues with Dink, Josh, and Ruth Rose
in their next exciting adventure!

The Canary Caper

Turn the page to start reading!

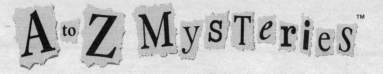

A to Z Mysteries

The Canary Caper

by **Ron Roy**

**illustrated by
John Steven Gurney**

A STEPPING STONE BOOK™

Random House New York

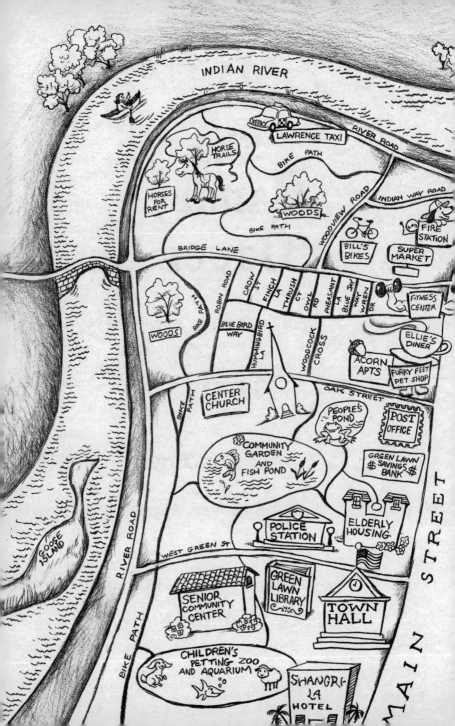

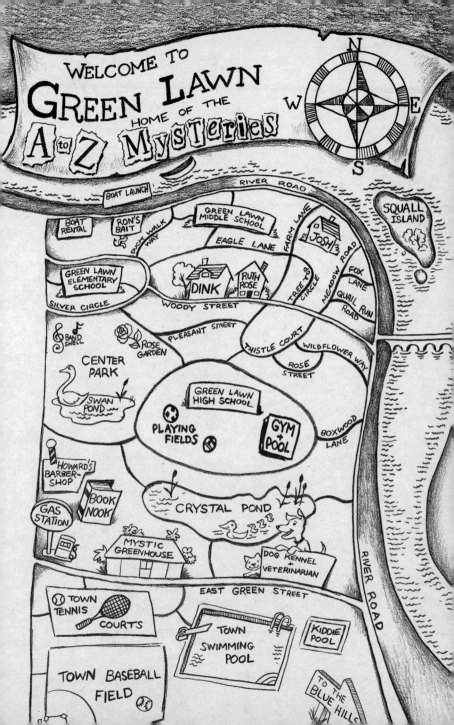

Chapter 1

Dink Duncan opened his front door. His best friend, Josh Pinto, was standing on the steps. "Hi, Josh. C'mon in," said Dink. "I just finished lunch."

Josh hurried past Dink, wiping his forehead. "We sure picked the hottest day of the summer to go to the circus," he said. "I just took a shower, and I'm still hot."

Dink grinned. "You took a shower? Let's see, that's two showers this month, right?"

"Haw haw, very funny," Josh said. He opened the refrigerator door and pulled up his shirt. "Ahh, that feels good!"

"It won't feel so good if my mom catches you," Dink said.

Josh grabbed the apple juice and flopped into a chair. "You're funny, but it's too hot to laugh," he said, pouring himself a glass. "Where's Ruth Rose? It's almost time to leave."

"She's waiting next door." Dink put his plate in the sink. "I have to run up and brush my teeth."

"Forget your teeth—the circus is waiting!"

Dink grinned and pointed to a clown-faced cookie jar on the counter. "Grab a cookie. I'll be right down."

Josh made a beeline for the cookie jar. "Take your time brushing," he said.

"Don't eat all of them!" Dink said, leaping up the stairs.

"Dink," his mother called, "are you running?"

"Sorry, Mom," he called back. "We're in a hurry. Thursday is half-price admission if we get to the circus by one o'clock."

Dink brushed his teeth, yanked a comb through his blond hair, then charged back down the stairs.

"Donald David Duncan!" his mother yelled. "No running in the house!"

The phone rang in the kitchen.

"Got it, Mom!" Dink grabbed the phone, watching Josh stuff a whole cookie into his mouth. "Hello, Duncan residence."

Dink listened, then said, "We'll be over in five minutes." He hung up.

"We'll be over where in five minutes?" Josh asked.

"Mrs. Davis's house. You know her canary, Mozart? He's escaped."

"What about the circus?" asked Josh. "Half-price, remember?"

Dink shrugged. "So we pay full price. Mrs. Davis needs our help."

They walked next door to Ruth Rose's house and rang the bell. Four-year-old Nate Hathaway opened the door. He stared up at Dink with huge blue eyes.

"Hi, Natie," said Dink. "Is Ruth Rose ready?"

Nate's lips, cheeks, and T-shirt were smeared with chocolate. He was holding a raggedy stuffed dinosaur.

"Sheef ungt fruz," Nate said with a full mouth.

Dink laughed. "She's *what?*"

Ruth Rose showed up behind Nate.

"MOM, WE'RE LEAVING NOW!" she screamed into the house.

Josh clapped both hands over his ears. "Ruth Rose, you should get a job as a car salesman. Then you could yell all day and get paid for it."

Ruth Rose stepped outside and closed the door. "You know perfectly well that I'm going to be President," she said sweetly. "And it's sales*woman*, Josh."

Ruth Rose liked to dress in one color. Today it was purple, from her sneakers to the headband holding back her black curls.

While they walked down Woody Street, Dink told Ruth Rose about Mrs. Davis's missing canary.

"Mozart got out of his cage?" Ruth Rose said. "I hope he doesn't fly over here. Tiger could swallow a canary in one bite."

"Your fat cat could swallow a turkey in one bite," Josh said.

Ruth Rose rolled her eyes. "Tiger is plump," she said, "not fat. Race you!"

Mrs. Davis was standing in the doorway of her large yellow house when they arrived. "Thank you for coming right over," she said.

Mrs. Davis held a handkerchief, and her eyes were red. "I didn't know who else to call."

"We don't mind," Dink said. "What happened to Mozart?"

"After breakfast, I hung his cage out back so he could have some fresh air. But when I went to give him his lunch, his cage was empty!"

"I'm sure he's somewhere nearby. Don't worry!" Dink said.

Dink, Josh, and Ruth Rose ran around to the backyard. Mozart's cage was hanging in an apple tree.

"Split up," Dink said. "Check all the bushes and flowers."

The kids searched every tree, shrub, and flower bed. Mrs. Davis watched from her back porch. "Any luck?" she asked Dink.

He shook his head. "I'm afraid not, but we'll keep looking."

"It's such a beautiful day," Mrs. Davis said. "I hope you kids have something fun planned."

"After we find Mozart, we're going to the circus," Dink told her.

"The circus! Well, please don't let me stop you!" Mrs. Davis said. "Mozart knows his cage. I'm sure he'll fly home soon."

But Dink could tell that Mrs. Davis wasn't really so sure. "Okay, but we'll call you later," he promised.

They said good-bye to Mrs. Davis and headed for the high school. The

Tinker Town Traveling Circus had set up on the school baseball field the day before and would leave town Monday night.

The kids cut through a bunch of circus trailers and trucks on their way to the admissions gate. The sides of the trailers were painted with pictures of clowns, tigers, and elephants.

They arrived five minutes after one, but the ticket lady let them in for half-price anyway, a dollar each.

"What'll we do first?" Ruth Rose asked.

"Let's eat," Josh said.

"No way," Dink said. "You already had lunch, and you probably gobbled down half my mom's cookies. Let's walk around and see what's here."

They watched birds do tricks, dogs ride on ponies, and a chimp dressed like Elvis "sing" into a microphone.

They all gulped when a tiger trainer
put his hand right inside a tiger's
mouth.

"Guess the tiger's not hungry," Josh
said with a grin.

In Clown Corner, a clown dressed as a giraffe danced on stilts. He kept time to the music by snapping his yellow suspenders.

"I have to leave soon," Ruth Rose

said after a while. "My mom needs me to watch Nate while she goes shopping."

The kids left, cutting through the town rose garden to get to Woody Street.

Dink snapped his fingers. "I just remembered—my mom said I can set up my tent in the backyard. Can you guys get permission to sleep out?"

"No problem for me," Josh said.

"Nate's never slept in a tent, so I'll bring him," Ruth Rose said. "And Tiger," she added sweetly.

"Your little brother!" Josh yelped. "Great, we'll have our own circus—a four-year-old monkey and a man-eating tiger!"

Ruth Rose laughed. "Don't worry. We'll bring our own tent."

Dink and Josh dropped Ruth Rose off at her house, then continued on to

Dink's. There they went inside and called Mrs. Davis.

"She says Mozart hasn't come back," Dink told Josh after he'd hung up.

While they were pitching Dink's tent, Ruth Rose came over. Nate trailed behind her, dragging his extinct-looking stuffed dinosaur.

"Hey, where's your man-eating cat?" Josh asked.

Ruth Rose dropped her tent on the ground. She looked as if she'd just swallowed something nasty.

"What's the matter, Ruth Rose?" Dink asked.

"Tiger is missing," Ruth Rose said quietly. "And my mother says she hasn't been home all day."

Chapter 2

Early the next morning, Ruth Rose poked her head into Dink's tent. "Wake up, you guys!"

Dink shot up out of a sound sleep. "Did Tiger come back?" he asked, peering sleepily at Ruth Rose.

"No, she didn't. I'm going to the police station and I want you guys to come with me."

Josh rolled over in his sleeping bag. "To report a missing cat?"

"No, to report a missing cat *and* a missing canary," Ruth Rose said. Then she ducked back out of the tent.

Dink and Josh looked at each other, then crawled out after her. Ruth Rose was pacing back and forth across the lawn.

"Guys, it's just too weird," she said. "Two animals disappeared from the same street on the same day!" Ruth Rose stopped pacing and looked at them. "I don't think Mozart and Tiger wandered off, I think they were stolen. I'm taking Nate home, and then you guys are coming with me to talk to Officer Fallon."

Ruth Rose woke up Nate, took his hand, and marched toward her house.

Dink and Josh just looked at each other and shrugged. Then they walked into Dink's house. Josh poured two bowls of cereal while Dink ran up to his room to change. Loretta, his guinea pig, squeaked a hello to Dink from her cage.

Josh was slurping up his Weet Treets when Dink came back down.

"I've been thinking," Josh said. "Wouldn't Tiger eat Mozart if someone kidnapped them both?"

Dink shrugged. "I don't know. I'm not even sure that Tiger and Mozart were kidnapped," he said between bites. "But Ruth Rose is our friend, so let's go to the police station with her."

Ruth Rose walked in wearing blue shorts and a red shirt. "You guys ready to go?" she asked.

Dink stared. He'd never seen Ruth Rose wear two different colors at the same time. He gave Josh a look, but Josh was busy reading the back of the cereal box and didn't notice.

"Yup, we're ready," Dink said, putting the bowls and glasses in the sink.

They found Officer Fallon at his desk. He was typing at his computer, chewing gum, and sipping tea all at the same time.

"Well, hi, gang," he said, smiling at the kids. "Going to the circus this weekend? How about some free passes?"

"No thanks, we went yesterday," Dink said.

Officer Fallon handed Josh three tickets. "Go again, on the Green Lawn Police!"

"Officer Fallon, I have a problem," Ruth Rose said.

He pointed at some chairs. "Have a seat. I'm all ears."

"It's my cat, Tiger. She's been gone for a whole day and night," Ruth Rose said. "She's never been away from home that long! Mrs. Davis's canary disappeared, too!"

Dink had never seen Ruth Rose look or sound so serious.

Officer Fallon wrote something on a sheet of paper.

"I think someone in Green Lawn is stealing pets," Ruth Rose went on. "Two pets vanishing on the same day is just too weird!"

"Four pets," Officer Fallon said. He opened his drawer and pulled out a sheet of paper. "Four pets are missing."

"Four?" Dink and Josh said together.

Officer Fallon nodded. "Last night, Dr. Pardue called. His kids' rabbit was missing from its cage. Later, Mrs. Gwynn called. It seems her parrot disappeared off her back porch."

"All yesterday?" Dink asked.

Officer Fallon nodded.

"I was right!" Ruth Rose said, jumping to her feet. "There *is* a pet-napper around here!"

"Four animals disappearing on the same day does seem strange," Officer Fallon said. "In fact, I've already asked Officer Keene to look into it."

He looked at Ruth Rose. "Could it be that your cat just took a little vacation, Ruth Rose? I used to have a cat who was a real wanderer."

"Well, Tiger isn't," Ruth Rose answered firmly.

Officer Fallon nodded. He told the kids he'd let them know if he discovered anything.

The kids left the police station and walked toward Main Street.

"Sounds like you might be right, Ruth Rose," Dink said.

"Maybe we should go see Mrs. Wong, just in case," Josh suggested. "People always bring her stray animals. Maybe someone found Tiger and brought her to the pet shop."

Ruth Rose rewarded Josh with a huge smile. "Great idea, Josh!"

They passed Howard's Barbershop. Howard was out front, sweeping his sidewalk.

"Have you seen my big orange cat?" Ruth Rose called.

Howard shook his head. "Sorry, Ruth Rose."

At the Furry Feet pet shop, Mrs.

Wong told Ruth Rose the same thing. "Nobody brought Tiger in," she said. "But I'll keep my eyes peeled."

"Mrs. Davis's canary is gone, too," Dink told Mrs. Wong.

"And Dr. Pardue's rabbit and Mrs. Gwynn's parrot!" Josh said.

"Four animals are missing? That *is* very strange!" Mrs. Wong glanced around her shop. "I guess I should count my own critters!"

"May I use your phone, Mrs. Wong?" Ruth Rose asked. "I want to call my mom and see if Tiger's home yet."

"Help yourself," Mrs. Wong said.

Ruth Rose dialed, spoke quietly to her mother, then hung up.

"Tiger's still gone," she said. "Who'd want to steal a canary, a cat, a parrot, and a rabbit?"

"I don't know," Dink said. "But we're going to find out!"

Chapter 3

The kids left the pet shop and headed up Main Street. They walked slowly, thinking about what to do.

"I've read about scientists stealing animals to use in experiments," Josh said.

"That's awful!" Dink said.

"I don't want Tiger used in some

experiment!" said Ruth Rose. "We have to find those animals. Where do the Gwynns and the Pardues live?"

"The Gwynns live over by us, on Thistle Court," Dink said.

"Why don't we go talk to them?" Ruth Rose said. "Maybe the pet-napper left some clues."

The kids cut through the high school grounds and passed the circus trailers. A few of the workers were sitting at a picnic table drinking coffee. They waved when the kids walked by.

"Which house is the Gwynns'?" Ruth Rose asked when they reached Thistle Court.

"That big gray one," Josh said. The mailbox in front said GWYNN in black letters.

Ruth Rose walked up the steps and rang the doorbell. Mrs. Gwynn opened the door.

"Hi, kids! How's your summer so far?" she asked.

"Not so great," Ruth Rose said. "Someone stole my cat yesterday."

"Oh, Ruth Rose, how awful! My parrot disappeared yesterday, too!"

"So did Mrs. Davis's canary," Josh added.

"We just came from the police station," Dink put in. "Officer Fallon told us about your parrot. Dr. Pardue's rabbit is also missing."

Mrs. Gwynn's mouth fell open. "My goodness! Do you mean that four pets disappeared yesterday?"

"We think so," Ruth Rose said. "Where was your parrot when you last saw him?"

"On my back porch, in his cage," Mrs. Gwynn said.

"Can we see the cage?" Dink asked.

Mrs. Gwynn took them through the

kitchen to a screened-in back porch. A cage stood in one corner.

"Archie likes it out here," said Mrs. Gwynn. "He can watch the other birds in the trees. Yesterday I came out to have my lunch, but he was gone."

Dink checked the screen door that led to the backyard. "Was this locked?" he asked.

"I don't really remember. We often leave it unlocked," Mrs. Gwynn said.

"Could Archie have opened his cage door himself?" Josh asked.

Mrs. Gwynn shook her head. "We always keep a clothespin on his door to make sure he can't open it."

"So someone must have stolen him," Ruth Rose said.

"Oh, dear, I don't like to think of crime in Green Lawn," Mrs. Gwynn said with a sigh. "Can I offer you kids something to drink? It's pretty warm."

"No thanks," Ruth Rose said. "But do you mind if we look in your phone book for Dr. Pardue's address?"

"They're at number three Pheasant Lane," Mrs. Gwynn said. "I drop Mike off there to play tennis with Andy Pardue."

The kids thanked Mrs. Gwynn and hurried to Main Street.

"This is getting weirder and weirder," Dink said. "A canary and a parrot were snatched right out of their cages in broad daylight. With people home!"

"And Tiger was probably in my backyard when she was taken," Ruth Rose said.

They waved to Mr. Paskey at the Book Nook and headed up Aviary Way. Three Pheasant Lane was a big green house surrounded by tall trees. A kid holding a tennis racket was sitting on the front porch.

"Hi," Ruth Rose said, walking up to the porch. "Is Dr. Pardue home? We'd like to talk to him about his rabbit."

"I'm Andy Pardue," the kid said. "Violet's my rabbit. Why? Did you find her?"

"No, but my cat is missing, too," Ruth Rose said. "And so are two other pets in town."

Dink glanced around the Pardues' front yard. "When did your rabbit disappear?" he asked Andy.

"After lunch yesterday," he said. "My sister ran into the house screaming. I went out to the cage, and the door was wide open. Violet was gone."

"Can you show us the cage?" Ruth Rose asked.

Andy led them to the backyard. An empty rabbit hutch stood under a tree.

"Was the cage locked?" Josh asked.

"Yep, I lock it every night myself."

Andy Pardue gave them a sharp look. "What's going on, anyway? A ring of animal thieves?"

"That's what we're trying to find out," Dink said.

"Well, let me know what you dig up," said Andy. "Boy, I'd like to get my hands on the creep who did this. My little sister cried all night!"

The kids walked back to Woody Street.

"Let's stop and check in with Mrs. Davis," Dink suggested as they passed her house. "We should tell her about the other missing animals."

When Mrs. Davis opened her door, she had a big smile on her face.

"Oh, I'm so glad to see you three!" she exclaimed. "You'll never guess! A man just called. He said he found Mozart! He's bringing him here at six-thirty. Isn't that lovely?"

"That's great." Dink looked at Josh and Ruth Rose in surprise.

"I want you three to be here, since you were kind enough to look for him," Mrs. Davis continued. "Afterward, we'll have some of my strawberry shortcake to celebrate!"

"Super!" Josh said.

"We'll see you at six-thirty," Dink said with a wave.

The three started home.

Josh grinned. "I guess Mozart wasn't kidnapped after all."

"I guess not," Dink said. He looked at Ruth Rose. She wasn't smiling.

"There's one thing I don't understand," she finally said. "How did he know who to call? How did that man know who Mozart belonged to?"

Dink shrugged. "Maybe he found him near Mrs. Davis's house and asked one of her neighbors."

"Or," Ruth Rose said, "maybe the guy who called is the same guy who *took* Mozart."

"But that doesn't make sense," Dink said. "Why would someone steal a canary on Thursday and return it the next day?"

"For the reward," Ruth Rose said with a frown. "This guy steals pets, then returns them for money."

Dink and Josh just stared at Ruth Rose.

They walked the rest of the way home in silence.

Chapter 4

Dink and Ruth Rose sat on Dink's front porch. They'd just finished dinner and were waiting for Josh.

Ruth Rose sighed.

"Tiger hasn't come home yet?" Dink asked.

She shook her head.

"Cats can be pretty mysterious sometimes," Dink said. He wanted Ruth Rose to feel better. "Maybe she's visiting a cat buddy somewhere."

Ruth Rose looked down. "She's never stayed away like this."

Suddenly Dink noticed that Ruth Rose had forgotten her headband. Her curly hair was hanging in her eyes.

Just then Josh came running down Woody Street, carrying his sketch pad. He jogged across Dink's lawn.

"Did Tiger come back yet?" he asked.

"No," Ruth Rose said, standing up. "Come on, let's go see who brings Mozart back."

A few minutes later, they were ringing Mrs. Davis's doorbell. Ruth Rose had a determined look in her eye. "If this guy has cat scratches on his hands, I'm calling Officer Fallon."

Mrs. Davis opened her door dressed for the occasion. The green gem in her necklace sparkled in the evening sunlight.

"I hope you've brought your appetites," she said. "To help us celebrate

Mozart's return, I've made some short-cake."

Josh grinned. "I might be able to eat a small helping."

Mrs. Davis laughed. "Oh, pooh, Joshua Pinto. I've seen what you can do to a batch of my cookies."

They walked into the living room. Mozart's empty cage sat on the piano.

"It will be so good to hear Mozart sing again," Mrs. Davis said.

The doorbell chimed. "He's here!" Mrs. Davis hurried to the door.

A thin young man stood smiling on the front porch. He was dressed neatly in a white shirt, dark pants, and blue suspenders.

The man held a small box with holes poked in the sides. "I'm Fred Little," he said. "Here's your canary."

Dink looked at the man's hands as he passed the box to Mrs. Davis. Not a

single claw mark. He shot a look at
Ruth Rose.

"Thank you, Mr. Little," said Mrs.
Davis. "Won't you step inside?"

Mrs. Davis introduced him to Dink,
Josh, and Ruth Rose. Then she opened
the box and lifted out her canary.

"Well, Mozart, how was your vacation?" She gave the canary a quick kiss and placed him in his cage.

Everyone paused to watch Mozart hop around, then settle down to preen his feathers.

"Mr. Little, I can't tell you how grateful I am," Mrs. Davis said. "But how did you know where to bring him?"

Ruth Rose kicked Dink in the ankle.

Fred Little smiled. "I had to do some detective work," he said. "I called the pet shop today and asked who in town owned a canary. A nice woman told me your name, so I looked you up in the phone book."

"That must have been Mrs. Wong," Dink said. "We talked to her today, too. About Ruth Rose's missing cat. When did you call her?"

The man stared at Dink. "I don't remember exactly," he said. "It was right after I caught the canary."

Mrs. Davis clapped her hands. "How thoughtful of you to go to so much trouble! Will you accept a reward?"

Ruth Rose glanced at Dink with a smirk on her face.

The man smiled at Mrs. Davis. "You're very kind," he said. "But no thanks. It's reward enough seeing your little bird back home again."

Dink snuck a quick look at Ruth Rose. She looked confused, and Dink could understand why.

If he won't take a reward, then he didn't steal Mozart. And if Mozart didn't get kidnapped, maybe Tiger didn't either, Dink thought.

"Then will you at least have a cup of tea and a cookie?" Mrs. Davis asked.

"That'll be fine," he said. "May I use your bathroom?"

"Down the hall on the right," Mrs. Davis said. "Kids, will you help me in the kitchen?"

While Mrs. Davis boiled water and arranged her silver tea service, the kids put cookies on a tray.

"He didn't take the reward," Ruth Rose whispered, frowning. "I can't believe I was wrong!"

"I don't know, Ruth Rose," Dink said. "There's something fishy about this guy. Why didn't Mrs. Wong tell us he called her?"

"We saw Mrs. Wong in the morning," Josh reminded them. "Fred Little must have called her later."

"Yeah, I suppose," Dink said.

"But I have this weird feeling I've seen Fred Little somewhere before," Josh said.

"Around here?" Ruth Rose asked.

Josh shrugged. "I'm not sure. I can't remember."

"What are you three whispering about?" Mrs. Davis called. "I'll need some helping hands in a minute."

When they were all seated around the card table, Mrs. Davis poured five cups of tea. "Are you just passing through, Mr. Little? I haven't seen you in town before."

"I'm here looking for a job," Fred Little said.

"So you might settle in Green Lawn? Wouldn't that be wonderful!"

Fred Little smiled. "It's a nice town." He glanced around the living room. "You sure have a lovely home, Mrs. Davis."

"Why, thank you. When my husband was alive, we traveled a great deal," Mrs. Davis said. "We brought back something special from each country we visited."

Fred Little left a few minutes later, and the kids helped Mrs. Davis clean up. "Still have room for shortcake?" she asked, grinning at Josh.

"Sure do!" he answered, picking up his sketch pad.

Josh began to draw a picture of Fred Little's face. "I just wish I could remember where I've seen this guy before."

Chapter 5

That night, a thunderstorm sent the kids running from their tents into their houses.

It was still raining the next day, so they decided to play Monopoly at Dink's house.

"Ruth Rose, it's your turn," Josh said.

"I know," she said, staring out Dink's window. "I can't concentrate. Tiger is out there in the rain."

Dink and Josh just looked at each other.

"If Fred Little didn't take the pets, then who could it be?" Ruth Rose asked. She came and plopped herself down at the Monopoly board.

Dink thought a moment. "If we could figure out *why* someone was stealing animals," he said, "maybe we could figure out *who* was doing it."

Ruth Rose picked up her stack of Monopoly cash. "I still think it's for money," she said. "When people get kidnapped, it's usually for ransom money, right?"

The boys nodded.

"But no one who's lost a pet has gotten a ransom note," Josh said.

"Not yet, anyway." Ruth Rose tossed her play money onto the table. "I'm going home. Mom put an ad in the paper, and I want to be there if anyone calls about Tiger."

The two boys watched her put on

her coat and head out into the rain.

"I've never seen her act so mopey," Josh said after the door closed. "She doesn't even argue with me anymore!"

"Yeah, and have you noticed she's not wearing one color either?" Dink pointed out. "I hope Tiger comes home soon."

That night the rain cleared up, so Dink and Josh slept out in the tent again.

The next morning, Ruth Rose woke them up. She was wearing cut-off jeans and an old T-shirt. Her untied sneaker laces were muddy from dragging.

"Read this, guys," she said, and she shoved the Sunday Morning Gazette under Dink's nose.

One paragraph was circled in red crayon. Dink and Josh stumbled out of the tent and sat at the picnic table.

The paragraph was under LOCAL

AREA CRIMES. Dink scanned it quickly, then read it out loud:

"Two Green Lawn homes were burglarized last night, Officer Charles Fallon has reported. The homes of Dr. and Mrs. Michael Pardue and Mr. and Mrs. Harvey Gwynn were entered by persons unknown. Several items of value were taken. Police are investigating."

Dink looked up. "Wow! First they lose their pets, then someone breaks into their houses. I think that stinks!"

"And I think they're connected," Ruth Rose said. "Don't you see, it *is* about money! Someone is taking pets, then breaking into the same houses."

"But why would someone need to steal a pet before robbing a house?" Dink asked.

"And not only that," Josh added, "but what about you and Mrs. Davis?

Your pets disappeared, but your houses weren't broken into."

"He's right, Ruth Rose," Dink said. "Why just two houses and not all four?"

Ruth Rose frowned at Dink and Josh. "I don't know," she said.

"We should try and find out. Let's go see the Pardues and the Gwynns again. Maybe the burglars left some clues!"

They hurried over to Thistle Court and rang the bell. Mr. Gwynn came to the door in his bathrobe.

"Oh, hi, kids! Mrs. Gwynn told me you stopped by Friday. Guess what? Yesterday afternoon, someone found our parrot and returned him!"

Ruth Rose stared at Mr. Gwynn. "Archie was returned yesterday?"

Mr. Gwynn nodded. "To celebrate, I took the family out for dinner and a movie. But when we got back home, we

discovered we'd been robbed. The rats took my coin collection."

"I'm sorry to hear that," Dink said.

"May I ask who returned your parrot?"

"A nice young woman," Mr. Gwynn told the kids. "She said she'd caught Archie eating seeds under her bird feeder."

"Did you invite her into your house?" Ruth Rose asked.

Before he could answer, Dink blurted out, "Did she see your coin collection?"

Mr. Gwynn's mouth dropped open. "Are you suggesting...Oh, my, you could be right!" he said. "The collection was in the living room where we sat and talked. Do you think she came back and stole it?"

Dink, Josh, and Ruth Rose looked at one another. Ruth Rose had her "I told you so!" look on her face.

"It sure seems that way, Mr. Gwynn," Dink said.

The kids thanked Mr. Gwynn, then raced all the way to the Pardues' house. Out of breath, Ruth Rose rang the bell.

Mrs. Pardue came to the door. "Hi, gang, what's up?" she said.

Ruth Rose asked, "By any chance, did someone bring your rabbit back yesterday, before your house got robbed?"

"Why, how did you know?" Mrs. Pardue asked. "A nice young couple called and said they'd found Violet in their garden. They brought her home yesterday afternoon."

Dink explained how the Gwynns' parrot had also been returned before they were robbed.

Mrs. Pardue's eyes got wide. "Of course! That couple came in and had a cold drink with us. Dr. Pardue offered them a reward, but they refused it."

"What did they steal?" Josh asked.

"Several pieces of my good jewelry," Mrs. Pardue said. "Some of it was left to me by my grandmother."

Ruth Rose thought for a minute. "Did they ask to use your bathroom?"

"Yes, the woman did," Mrs. Pardue answered. "She could have snooped in my bedroom at the same time. I feel so foolish!"

The kids said good-bye and headed for Main Street.

"I knew it!" Ruth Rose said. "The pet-nappers and the robbers are the same people!"

"Boy, what a dirty scam," Josh said. "You steal someone's pet, return it to get a guided tour of the place, then come back later to take what you liked."

"Talk about a double whammy," Dink said, shaking his head.

"I think it's gonna be a triple whammy," Ruth Rose said. "What about Mrs. Davis?"

"What about her?" Josh asked. "She hasn't...oh, my gosh!"

"That's right," Ruth Rose said. "I'll bet anything that Mrs. Davis's house is next!"

Chapter 6

"Or *your* house could be next," Dink reminded Ruth Rose.

Ruth Rose shook her head. "They didn't return Tiger, so they didn't get inside my house. Come on, we have to tell Officer Fallon!"

They ran down Main Street to the police station.

"Does he work on Sunday morning?" Josh asked as they hurried up the steps.

"We'll find out in a minute," Dink said.

The kids almost bumped into Officer Fallon coming through the door.

"Were you kids coming to see me?" he asked. "I was just heading for Ellie's."

"Officer Fallon, we figured out the burglaries!" Ruth Rose cried.

He looked at her. "Oh? Then we'd better go back inside."

Sitting at his desk, Officer Fallon picked up a pencil. "I'm listening," he said.

Ruth Rose told him their theory about how the pet-nappers came back later to return the animals, then rob the houses.

Officer Fallon smiled. "I think you're right on the button," he said. "I figured out the same thing."

"Did you know that Mrs. Davis's canary was returned, too?" Ruth Rose asked. She looked at Dink and Josh.

"We think *her* house will be robbed next!"

Officer Fallon raised his eyebrows. "Well, now, that *is* news. I didn't know about the canary. When was it returned?" he asked, writing something on his pad.

"Friday night," Josh said. "Some guy called up and said he'd found Mozart. He brought him over while we were there."

Officer Fallon's eyes widened. "Tell me about this man, Josh," he said quietly.

Josh described Fred Little while Officer Fallon took more notes.

"Can you arrest Fred Little before he breaks into Mrs. Davis's house?" Ruth Rose asked.

Officer Fallon tapped his pencil and squinted one eye at the kids. "Officer Keene and I have been looking for whoever returned the Gywnn and Pardue pets. We want to question them about the pet-nappings and the robberies. Now we will start looking for Fred Little, too."

He leaned forward on his elbows. "But we have no evidence that these people have done anything wrong. The same goes for Fred Little. True, he returned the canary and got inside Leona Davis's house. That's the same pattern as the other two burglaries, but it's not a crime."

"You can't arrest him?" Josh asked.

Officer Fallon shook his head. "Even if I knew where to find Fred Little, I have no proof that he's planning a crime."

"But we have to do something!" Ruth Rose said.

"You've already done a lot," Officer Fallon said. "I didn't know that Leona

Davis got her bird back. You've given me a good lead. Officer Keene and I really appreciate your help, kids."

He walked them to the door. "Don't worry, we have a few tricks up our sleeves."

"I still think we should do *something*," Ruth Rose said when they were outside.

"Well..." Josh said. "The circus is leaving tomorrow, and we do have those free tickets Officer Fallon gave us..."

Dink laughed. Together, he and Josh talked Ruth Rose into visiting the circus for a few hours.

They watched a few animal acts and bought popcorn.

Ruth Rose didn't feel like going on any rides, so they decided to go into the clown tent again.

Two clowns dressed as firefighters

were running around, bumping into each other while a small cardboard building "burned."

Smoke and fake flames were shooting out of a window. A woman clown was screaming, "Help! Save me!"

Some of the kids in the audience started yelling, "Save her, mister! Up there, save her!"

The firefighter clowns got tangled up in their own hoses, making everyone laugh and yell even louder.

Suddenly a clown dressed like Superman appeared on stilts. He wore a blue shirt under a red cape. Bright yellow suspenders held up the skinny blue pants that hid his stilts.

Superman flapped his cape and snapped his suspenders. Then he marched over to the burning tower and saved the woman. All the kids in the audience yelled and clapped.

Dink noticed that Ruth Rose was hardly even looking. He nudged Josh, and they left.

"I'd like to get me some stilts," Josh said. He walked stiff-legged and snapped invisible suspenders. "Do circuses ever hire kids?"

"Yeah, to feed to the tigers," Dink said, which reminded him of Ruth Rose's Tiger. He looked at her. "Do you want to come over and finish the Monopoly game?"

She shook her head. "Don't you guys want to solve this mystery?"

"Sure, but what else can we do?" Dink asked. "Officer Fallon said he's gonna look for the people who returned the pets."

"Well, I know how we can help him," Ruth Rose said, her eyes flashing.

"Uh-oh," Josh mumbled.

"Um, Ruth Rose, I don't think Officer Fallon wants any more help," Dink said.

Ruth Rose ignored him. "Are you guys sleeping in the tent again tonight?" she asked.

Dink nodded. "I guess so. Why?"

Ruth Rose grinned mysteriously. "I promise to bring over some cookies if you promise to go somewhere with me."

"Where?" Dink asked. "And why do you have that sneaky look on your face?"

"Wear dark clothes," Ruth Rose said. "We're going to stake out Mrs. Davis's house!"

Chapter 7

"A stakeout?" Josh said.

Ruth Rose nodded.

"Like in the cop movies?" Dink asked.

She nodded again.

"You think Mrs. Davis's house is going to get robbed tonight?" Josh said.

A third nod. "And I plan to be there to see who does it." She grinned. "Will that be enough proof for Officer Fallon?"

"Suppose a burglar does come," Dink said. "What do we do, tie him up?"

"All right!" Josh said. "I'll bring the rope."

Ruth Rose shook her head. "No rope. We just sit and watch. If someone comes, one of us will run to the police station. The other two will stay. If the guy leaves, we follow him."

Dink thought that over. "Follow him where?"

"Wherever he goes, Dink. Maybe he'll lead us to where he stashed the stuff he robbed," Ruth Rose said. "And maybe that's where he's got Tiger."

"Well, I guess it'll work, as long as we just watch the guy," Dink said.

Ruth Rose nodded. "We just wait and watch."

"And eat cookies," Josh added.

Dink and Josh sat in the dark tent, waiting for Ruth Rose. It was almost ten o'clock.

Josh wore camouflage pants and a black T-shirt. Dink had on jeans and a dark gray sweatshirt.

"Where the heck is she?" Josh asked.

Dink peeked out the tent flap. "My folks will kill me if we get caught running around Green Lawn at night."

"Mine would ground me for ten years," Josh said. "Why'd we let her talk us into this?"

Dink heard a noise. "Did you hear something?" he whispered.

Josh peeked out. "Ruth Rose? Is that you?"

"Boo!" Ruth Rose giggled. "I'm right here, Josh."

Dink poked his head out. He couldn't see a thing. "Come on, Ruth Rose, stop fooling around. Where are you hiding?"

"I'm not hiding!" Suddenly Dink

could see her. Ruth Rose was sitting about four feet away, right in front of him! She was wearing black jeans and a black jacket. Her hair was covered by a ski cap. She'd even blackened her face. Except for the whites of her eyes, Ruth Rose was practically invisible.

"What's that stuff on your face?" Dink asked.

"Liquid shoe polish." She pulled a bottle out of her backpack. "Here, put some on."

"Do we have to?" Dink said.

"Yes! What happens if the burglar sees your two white faces glowing in the moonlight?"

Dink poured some of the polish into his hand and smeared it all over his face. "This stuff stinks," he muttered.

Josh did the same. "I feel like Rambo," he said. Dink saw Josh's white teeth gleaming.

"Let's head out," Ruth Rose said, slipping away from the tent.

The boys followed her down Woody Street. Mrs. Davis's house was dark as they crept into her backyard. Dink tried not to think about what they were doing.

Ruth Rose chose their hiding place, a shadowy patch between two thick bushes behind the house.

The moon was almost full, but large clouds kept slipping in front of it. The kids wiggled around, getting comfortable on the lawn.

"Did you bring the cookies?" Josh asked.

"Yes, but let's save them till later," Ruth Rose said. "We might be here for hours."

Josh let out a big sigh. "People who break their promises..."

"She's right, Josh," Dink whispered.

"And I don't think we should talk anymore. If the burglar comes, he might hear us and take off."

Five seconds passed.

"One little cookie wouldn't kill you, Ruth Rose."

"Josh, this is a stakeout, not Ellie's Diner."

"Cops eat on stakeouts."

"JOSH! SHHH!"

Dink stretched out on the grass. He watched the back of the house for moving shadows. Nothing moved.

He slapped at a mosquito.

A white cat strolled through the yard.

Dink yawned.

Every few minutes, he checked his watch.

He closed his eyes.

When he opened them again, it was nearly eleven o'clock. Josh was sound asleep, but Dink could see that Ruth Rose's eyes were wide open.

"Are you hungry?" she whispered.

He nodded and shook Josh's shoulder.

Ruth Rose opened her pack. She brought out a bag of cookies, three bananas, and three cartons of apple juice.

They ate in silence, listening and watching for a burglar to show up.

"Thanks, Ruth Rose," Josh whispered. Then he lay back down and shut his eyes again.

Dink yawned and tried to get comfortable. He wished he'd brought his sleeping bag. It was soft and...suddenly he saw something move in the shadows next to the house.

He shook Josh and put his mouth next to Ruth Rose's ear. "Look," he whispered, pointing.

But whatever he'd seen wasn't moving now.

Dink trained his eyes on the back of the house. He saw only shadows of the trees and bushes.

Then one of the shadows moved.

Dink smelled Josh's cookie breath. "He's here!" Josh whispered. Dink could feel Josh trembling with excitement.

Dink's stomach did a quick plunge. Someone dressed in dark clothes and a

baseball cap was creeping behind Mrs.
Davis's house. He carried a gym bag
and a long pole. The prowler was in the
shadows, and Dink couldn't see his
face.

The burglar set his bag and the pole
on the ground. Then he checked each

first-floor window on the back of the house. Finding them all locked, he walked around the side, out of sight.

"What should we do?" Josh said. "Is he leaving?"

Dink shook his head. "He left his stuff."

"Did anyone recognize his face?" Ruth Rose asked.

Nobody had. Suddenly the dark figure returned. He stood with his back to them, looking up at the house.

Then the prowler turned around. He seemed to be looking directly at Dink.

Dink was glad he'd blackened his face. Suddenly Josh grabbed Dink's arm. "It's the canary guy!"

Ruth Rose let out a gasp.

Fred Little was walking right toward them!

Chapter 8

Dink tried to shrink into the dark space between the bushes. He could feel Josh and Ruth Rose doing the same.

His heart thudded as Fred Little stepped closer. Then he stopped, took off his jacket, and hung it on a tree branch three feet from Dink's nose. He walked back toward the house.

Josh grabbed Dink. "Look, he's wearing yellow suspenders!"

Dink remembered where he'd seen those suspenders. He grinned at Josh. "The Superman clown!"

"And the giraffe clown," Josh whispered back. "I *knew* I'd seen him before."

They watched as Fred Little opened his gym bag. He pulled out a coil of rope and looped it around his neck.

Then he picked up the long pole he'd brought with him. Only it wasn't a pole.

Fred Little had brought a pair of long stilts. He carefully leaned the stilts against the house and scooted up the foot rests. Now about ten feet tall, he stilt-walked to a spot under a small window on the second floor.

A moment later, Dink watched Fred Little slip through the window. First he was standing there on stilts, and then he was gone, like a snake slithering into a hole.

The stilts remained leaning against the side of the house.

Josh was at Dink's ear. "Should we—"

"Shhh, wait," Ruth Rose whispered.

Suddenly the rope uncoiled from the window. One end dangled to the ground, between the stilts.

"That must be how he's coming down," Ruth Rose said.

"Let's take the rope and stilts," Josh whispered. "He'll be trapped inside!"

"But Mrs. Davis is in there with him," Ruth Rose said. "We have to let him come out, then follow him."

"One of us should run to the police station now," Dink said.

The trouble was, no one wanted to leave the excitement.

Suddenly three things happened at once: The upstairs light blazed on. Dink heard a loud scream. A police whistle blared through the open window.

Dink leaped to his feet, not sure

what to do. Mrs. Davis was up there, and the burglar was probably in the same room with her!

But which one had let out that scream?

Dink saw a silhouette appear at the window. A second later, Fred Little was climbing down his escape rope. With his feet still above the ground, he dropped.

Suddenly the backyard exploded in color and noise.

A police cruiser roared across Mrs. Davis's lawn, flashing red, yellow, and blue lights. The backyard looked like a fireworks display.

The siren whooped loudly, shutting out the shrieking of the whistle.

Then the noise stopped as the cruiser doors burst open. Officers Fallon and Keene leaped out.

"Hold it!" Officer Fallon shouted.

Fred Little was still crouched on the ground where he had landed. Dink saw his mouth fall open in panic and surprise.

In seconds, he was wearing handcuffs.

As Officer Keene led the prisoner to the police car, the back door flew open. Mrs. Davis marched out in a white nightgown and floppy slippers. She flip-flopped across the yard toward Fred Little.

Her face was shiny with white cream. Some kind of lacy bonnet covered her hair. And she held a long sword high over her head.

"The nerve of you!" she yelled into Fred Little's terrified face. "Coming right into my bedroom!"

The sword flashed in the cruiser's headlights. Dink thought she was going to use it on the burglar!

"I heard you trying to find my jewelry!" she shouted. "And after I fed you
tea and cookies!"

"Come on," Ruth Rose said.

Everyone, but especially Fred Little,
was surprised to see three little ninjas
crawl out of the bushes.

Chapter 9

Ruth Rose stomped up to Fred Little and glared at him. "Where's my Tiger?" she demanded.

Fred Little backed away. "What tiger?"

"Tiger is my cat. Did you steal her? Where is she?"

"I didn't take any cat," he muttered. "I'm allergic to cats."

"What're you kids doing here?" Officer Fallon asked with a frown.

"We thought someone might try to break in tonight," Ruth Rose said, pointing at the prisoner. "We wanted to get proof so you could arrest him."

"This is Fred Little," Josh said. "The guy who returned Mrs. Davis's canary. He's also a clown in the circus."

"And he's probably the one who robbed Dr. Pardue's house and the Gwynns', too," Dink added.

"It certainly looks that way," Officer Fallon said. He gave instructions to Officer Keene, who locked Fred Little in the cruiser and drove away.

Officer Fallon looked sternly at Dink. "We'll talk tomorrow," he said. "You kids better skedaddle home and get some sleep."

"Fiddlesticks!" Mrs. Davis said. "These children won't perish if they stay up a little longer. And *I* won't sleep a wink! Come inside for cookies and cocoa, all of you."

Officer Fallon just smiled and shook his head as they followed Mrs. Davis into her kitchen. Dink noticed Mozart's cage sitting on the counter.

Mrs. Davis put water on to boil and took mugs from a cupboard. Then she pulled the cover off the birdcage. Mozart twittered and blinked his tiny black eyes.

"You've certainly put everyone through a lot of trouble," she told her canary.

"Actually, Leona, your canary helped us to solve a string of burglaries," Officer Fallon said. "I did some snooping and found out a lot about Fred Little and his girlfriend. They've been traveling with the circus, and robbing houses in the towns they visit, for quite some time. And they always do it the same way. First they steal pets. Then they return the pets to get a peek inside the houses. Later, they rob the same houses."

Mrs. Davis shook her head. "You should have seen that creepy man's face when I turned on the light. But how did he know I left my upstairs bathroom window open?"

"He probably saw that it was open when he took your canary," Officer Fallon said.

"Or maybe he left it open," Dink said. "He might have snuck upstairs when he used the bathroom."

"You could be right, Dink," Officer Fallon said. "On stilts, he could get into upstairs windows that most people leave unlocked. In the robbery business, he's known as a second-story man."

"After tonight," Mrs. Davis said, "that window will be locked!"

"How did you know that Fred Little would try to break in tonight?" Dink asked.

"We were parked right around the corner," Officer Fallon continued. "We figured the burglary had to be tonight or never, since the circus leaves town tomorrow."

Suddenly there was a knock at the door. Officer Fallon stood up and stretched. "That'll be Officer Keene back with the car. We'll drive you kids home now. I hope we didn't wreck your yard, Leona."

"Oh, pooh. You saved my jewelry and caught a pair of criminals," she said. "Besides, I know three children who might like to earn some money raking and planting grass seed."

Officer Fallon laughed. "You could have caught Fred Little all by yourself. Where'd that sword come from, Leona?"

"My husband brought it back from one of our trips," she said, smiling. "It's been under my bed for years, in case I ever needed it."

"Did you see that guy's face?" Josh asked. "I think he was glad to go to jail!"

Officer Fallon and Officer Keene dropped the kids off at Dink's house. "Good night, kids," Officer Fallon said. "No more sneaking around, okay?"

The kids promised they'd go right to bed and watched the cruiser drive away.

"I wonder if Fred Little was telling the truth about Tiger," Ruth Rose said. "All the pets got returned except mine."

"Tomorrow we'll help you search, right, Josh?" Dink said.

"Right," Josh said. "We'll ring every doorbell in Green Lawn if we have to."

Ruth Rose nodded, looking sad. "Thanks, guys."

The boys said good night to Ruth

Rose, then walked around back and crawled into their tent.

Josh giggled in the dark. "Did you see Mrs. Davis come flying out her door with all that goop on her face? I thought she was a ghost!"

Dink grinned. "Yeah, and old Fred Little came shooting out the window like a rocket. I bet he burned his hands sliding down that rope."

Dink rolled over and closed his eyes.

Thirty seconds later, Ruth Rose burst through the tent flap. She shined a flashlight into Dink's face.

"GUYS, WAKE UP!" she yelled.

Josh bolted straight up. "Geez, Ruth Rose, my heart can't take any more surprises tonight."

"What's wrong?" Dink asked, blinking.

"TIGER CAME HOME!" Ruth Rose

said, flopping down next to Dink's feet. "She was on my bed when I snuck upstairs. When I went to pick her up, she hopped down and crawled under the bed."

Ruth Rose grinned. "And guess what I found under there with her?"

"A sword?" Dink guessed.

"Nope!"

"A burglar?" Josh asked, blinking into the flashlight.

"No! I found three kittens. I'M A GRANDMOTHER!"

This is the end of

The Canary Caper

Collect clues with Dink, Josh, and Ruth Rose
in their next exciting adventure!

The Deadly Dungeon

Turn the page to start reading!

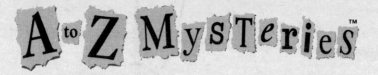

A to Z Mysteries™

The Deadly Dungeon

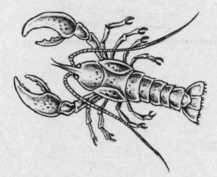

by **Ron Roy**

illustrated by
John Steven Gurney

A STEPPING STONE BOOK™

Random House 🏠 New York

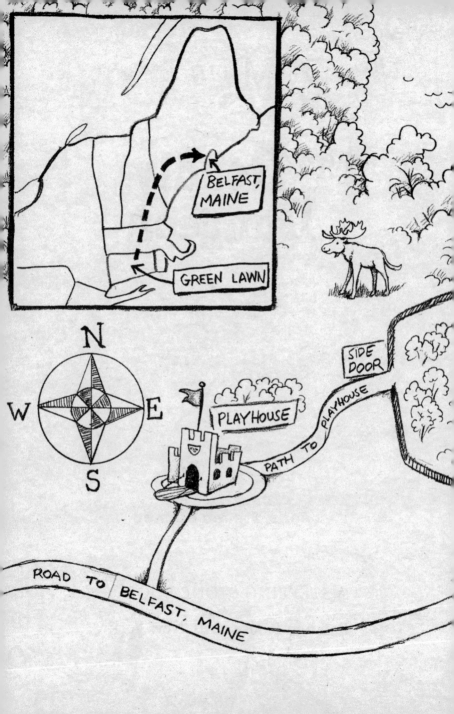

BELFAST, MAINE

GREEN LAWN

N

W E

S

PLAYHOUSE

SIDE DOOR

PATH TO PLAYHOUSE

ROAD TO BELFAST, MAINE

Chapter 1

Dink squirmed in his seat. He, Josh, and Ruth Rose had been riding the bus since seven that morning.

They were on their way to Maine to visit their friend Wallis Wallace, a famous mystery writer. The three of them had met her when she came to Green Lawn. Dink smiled when he remembered how they had rescued Wallis from a "kidnapper."

Dink glanced over at Josh, asleep in his seat. His sketch pad was open on his lap.

Behind Josh, Ruth Rose was looking at a map. She liked to dress in one color. Today it was green, from her T-shirt to her high-tops.

Dink moved into the seat next to Ruth Rose. "Where are we?" he asked.

"Almost there." She pointed to Belfast, Maine, on her map. "We just passed a Welcome to Belfast sign."

Dink nodded. That was where Wallis was picking them up.

Ruth Rose tucked her map into her pack. "I'm so excited!" she said. "Do you think her castle has a moat and a dungeon?"

"I just hope it has food," Dink said. "I'm starving!"

Josh's head popped up in front of them. "Me too! Are we there yet?"

Just then the bus driver called out, "Belfast!"

"All right!" Josh said, leaping into the aisle.

The bus stopped in front of a small gray-shingled building. Through the window, Dink could see the water.

"Do you see Wallis?" Ruth Rose asked.

Dink grabbed his pack. "No, but let's get off. I think I'm allergic to buses!"

The kids headed for the front. They followed an elderly couple down the steps.

They were squinting into the blinding sunlight when they heard someone say, "Hi, kids!" A tall man with curly blond hair was walking toward them. His face was tanned and smiling.

"I remember you. You're Wallis's brother!" Ruth Rose said.

"Call me Walker, okay?" said the

man. "Wallis is buying groceries, so she asked me to get you."

Walker Wallace picked up Dink's pack. It clunked heavily against his leg.

"What's in here, your rock collection?" he asked.

Dink grinned. "Books. My mom said it rains a lot in Maine, so I came prepared."

Walker laughed. "We've planned perfect weather for you guys. Sun every day! Come on, that's my Jeep over there."

Walker's dusty brown Jeep had no top. The leather seats were worn and split in places.

He swept a pair of boots and a tool belt onto the floor, making room in the backseat. "Pile in!"

The boys climbed into the back. Ruth Rose sat next to Walker. "How far is the castle?" she asked.

"Not far." Walker pointed. "About a mile past those trees."

He drove up the coast. "You guys hungry? Sis is buying everything in the store for you."

"I'm *always* hungry," Josh said, leaning back and crossing his legs. He took a deep breath of the ocean air. "What a smell!"

"I'll say," Dink said. "Get your smelly foot out of my face!"

"It's not smelly," Josh said, wiggling his sneaker under Dink's nose.

"What's this?" Dink plucked a bright green feather off the sole of Josh's sneaker.

Josh shrugged. "I must've picked it up on the bus."

Dink slipped the feather into his pocket.

"There's Moose Manor!" Walker called. He pointed through the trees.

Dink stared at the tall castle. It was
built of huge gray stones. Its small dark
windows looked like watching eyes. An
iron fence surrounded the building.

"Cool," Dink said softly.

"Look, guys, a moat!" Ruth Rose
said.

"And a drawbridge!" cried Josh.

Walker pulled up in front of the gate. The kids hopped out with their packs.

"I have to get back to my boat," Walker said. "Sis should be here soon. Have fun!" He waved and sped back through the trees.

Up close, the castle towered over the kids. The battlements on top reminded Dink of giant's teeth.

Josh pushed the gate, and it creaked open. They peered down into the moat. Ruth Rose let out a laugh. "Look, guys!"

The bottom of the empty moat was planted with flowers!

"Hey, guys!" Josh called. "Check this out!" He had crossed the drawbridge and was standing in front of an enormous wooden door. He tugged on the handle, but the door wouldn't budge. "How the heck does Wallis get in?"

Just then Dink heard a car. A red Volkswagen convertible zoomed up to the gate. The horn tooted, and a hand waved wildly.

"It's Wallis!" shouted Dink.

Chapter 2

"Welcome!" Wallis yelled.

She looked the same as Dink remembered: happy smile, curly brown hair, mischievous eyes.

"What do you think of Moose Manor?" she asked. "Isn't it fun?"

"I love it!" said Ruth Rose.

"It's awesome!" Josh said.

Wallis laughed. "It is something, isn't it? Help me with these groceries, and I'll take you on the grand tour!"

The entrance to the castle turned out to be a regular-sized door around the corner. Wallis and the kids carried bags of groceries into a large room. Dink saw a washer and dryer, wooden pegs for hats and coats, and a pile of sneakers and boots.

"This is my mud room," Wallis said. "The kitchen is through here." She shoved open another door with her hip.

Dink had to tip his head back to see the high ceiling. The usual kitchen stuff was there, with a long wooden table in the middle. A black chandelier hung over the table.

"This place is humongous!" Dink said.

"That's why I love it," Wallis said. "Let's put the food away and I'll show you around."

The kids quickly emptied the bags while Wallis put the milk and ice cream into the refrigerator.

"Okay, the tour begins in the royal

living room," Wallis said. "Follow me!" She led them into the biggest living room Dink had ever seen.

The first thing Dink noticed was the chandelier hanging right over his head. It was as big as Wallis's car!

A marble fireplace took up almost one whole wall. The mantel was dark wood, carved with all kinds of animals.

"This place is amazing!" Dink said.

"Geez," Josh breathed, peering into the fireplace. "You could burn a whole tree in here!"

Wallis flopped onto a pile of floor cushions. "Some winter days I wish I could," she said. "It gets mighty cold up on this cliff."

"How old is this place?" Ruth Rose asked, peering up at the tall stone walls.

"Pretty old," Wallis said. "It was built in the 1930s by a movie star named Emory Scott."

"Awesome!" Josh said.

"What happened to him?" Dink asked.

"Well..." Wallis raised her eyebrows and lowered her voice. "According to the town gossip, he died suddenly. Right here in the castle. In fact, sometimes I think I hear his ghost!"

The kids stared with open mouths.

Then Dink laughed. "Come on, you're just kidding, right?"

"Why? Don't you believe in ghosts?" Wallis asked with a grin.

"No way!" they all yelled.

"Well..." Wallis stood up. "Maybe Emory will introduce himself when he's ready. In the meantime, why don't I show you your rooms?"

The kids grabbed their packs and followed Wallis up a wide stone staircase to the second floor. At the top of the stairs was a dim hallway with several doors.

Wallis pointed to one. "That's my room. Ruth Rose, yours is there, and I've put you boys together, right across the hall."

Wallis tapped on a narrow door at the end of the hall. "This one leads up to the roof."

Dink opened the door to their bedroom. Like the rooms downstairs, the ceiling was high. A blue carpet covered the stone floor. The twin beds had bright red covers.

Dink went to the window and looked outside. All he could see were pine trees. "Where's the ocean?" he asked.

"On the other side," Wallis said. "Why don't you settle in, then come down for lunch?"

Ruth Rose went to her room. Dink and Josh dumped their packs on their beds.

"This place is so cool," Josh said, wandering into their bathroom.

Dink stacked his books on the table next to his bed. He pawed through his clothes, then changed into shorts and a T-shirt.

"Dink, come in here!" Josh called.

Dink wandered into the bathroom.

"Listen," Josh said. He had his ear against one of the bathroom walls.

"What're you doing?" asked Dink.

Josh made a shushing sound. "I thought I heard something!"

"What's going on?" Ruth Rose said as she came into the room.

"Josh thought he heard something behind the wall," Dink said.

Ruth Rose grinned. "It must be the ghost of Emory Scott. He's just waiting for you two to fall asleep tonight!"

Just then they heard Wallis's voice. "Come and get it!" she called. They raced down to the kitchen.

Wallis was packing a basket. "It's such a great day, I thought we'd have a picnic on the beach," she said.

"Cool!" Josh said. "Can we go fishing there sometime?"

Wallis nodded. "Ask Walker if you can borrow some gear. In fact, he's taking you lobstering tomorrow."

"Awesome!" Josh yelled.

Wallis smiled. "You won't think so at four-thirty tomorrow morning."

Dink and Josh each grabbed one end of the picnic basket. Wallis handed Ruth Rose a blanket, then led them to the back of the castle and through another gate.

"Great view, isn't it?" Wallis said. "The first time I saw this place, I knew I had to do my writing here."

Dink took a deep breath of the sea air. Small boats made colorful dots against the blue ocean. "It's really nice," he said.

Josh peered nervously over the cliff. "How do we get down?"

Wallis laughed. "See there? I had steps built. But poor Emory Scott! You remember that marble fireplace and that massive chandelier? Every piece came from Europe by boat. Goodness knows how he got them up this cliff!"

Suddenly a scream burst from the castle behind them.

Dink nearly dropped his end of the picnic basket. The skin on his arms erupted into a thousand goose bumps.

Wallis glanced back and grinned. "Dink, Josh, Ruth Rose, allow me to introduce...the ghost of Emory Scott!"

Chapter 3

The kids stared at Wallis in silence.

She winked at them. "Don't worry, that's just his way of saying hello. Shall we go down?"

The kids glanced at each other, then followed Wallis down the wooden stairs. At the bottom they found a small, sandy beach.

Dink and Josh set the basket in the shade of some boulders while Wallis and Ruth Rose spread the blanket.

"Look! A cave!" Josh said, pointing at a tunnel at the bottom of the cliff. The sea snaked into the dark hole, making a narrow river.

"How far does it go in?" Josh asked, peering into the black space.

"I don't know," Wallis said. "Walker

told me that it's full of bats."

They picnicked on chicken sandwiches, apples, chocolate chip cookies,
and cold lemonade. Wallis pointed
down the shoreline. "Walker's house is
beyond those trees."

"Where is he?" asked Dink.

"Out on his boat," Wallis said, waving a cookie at the ocean. "His lobster
pots are scattered over about a half mile
of very deep water."

"How does he find them?" Josh
asked.

Wallis wiped her fingers on a paper
napkin. "Well, he has a good compass
aboard *Lady Luck*—that's his boat—and
he knows the water."

After their picnic, Wallis put everything back into the basket. "Ready for a
walk?"

They hiked along the rocky beach.
Ruth Rose poked into tide pools and

picked up shells. Josh hung his sneakers around his neck and waded along the shore.

"Better watch out for lobsters," Dink teased. "They like smelly toes."

Josh grinned and splashed Dink.

Rounding a curve in the shoreline, Wallis pointed. "There's Walker's place."

It was a gray cottage with a red roof, surrounded by dune grass and sand.

Just then they heard a shout. Dink looked around and saw someone waving from the end of a dock.

Wallis waved back. "Kids, come and meet our friend Ripley Pearce."

They walked out on the dock toward a long green boat tied at the end. The boat's brass and wood trim gleamed in the sunlight.

A man stood next to the boat, holding a dripping sponge. He had dark slicked-back hair and blue eyes.

"Hi, Rip," Wallis said. "Meet Dink Duncan, Josh Pinto, and Ruth Rose Hathaway."

The man smiled and stuck out a hand. He had dazzling white teeth and a deep tan. "You're fans of this lady's books, right?"

"I've got all of them!" Dink announced.

"I met these three in Connecticut," Wallis explained. "They're spending a week up at the castle. Why don't you come for supper with us tonight?"

"I like your boat," Ruth Rose said. "It's so shiny and clean!"

Rip flashed her a grin. "Thank you very much, little lady. I'll see you tonight at dinner."

Then he looked at Josh. "Want to untie me?" he asked, pointing to a rope tied to the end of the dock.

Josh untied the rope and handed it to Rip.

"Nice meeting you kids," he said, stepping aboard his boat. He started the engine, and the boat pulled smoothly away from the dock.

Dink watched the boat cut through the water. "Maybe I won't be a writer when I grow up. Maybe I'll get a lobster boat."

Wallis grinned at Dink. "Better stick to writing, Dink. Lobsters are getting scarce in Maine."

"I can't wait to go out on Walker's boat," Ruth Rose said.

"My brother's boat is nothing like Rip's," Wallis said. She shook her head. "I don't know how Rip keeps his so clean. Walker's boat looks and smells like a lobster boat."

They walked back toward their picnic spot. Josh kicked water on Ruth

Rose, and she chased him down the beach, yelling all the way.

Dink walked quietly along with Wallis. Overhead, a sea gull cried out.

Dink looked up at Wallis. "Do you really think that scream we heard was the ghost of Emory Scott?"

Wallis laughed. "All I know is I've been hearing those screams since I moved in. The first time, I searched the castle. But I never found a thing."

Dink shivered. "Do you hear the noises a lot?" he asked.

Wallis shrugged. "Sometimes weeks go by and there's not a peep. Then I'll hear them for a few days in a row."

Wallis smiled down at Dink. "To tell you the truth, Dink, this is one mystery that's got me stumped. If those screams aren't the ghost of Emory Scott, I don't know what they are!"

Chapter 4

At the top of the cliff, Wallis took the picnic things. "I need to spend some time working on my new book," she said. "Why don't you guys go exploring? Emory Scott built a playhouse for his kids in those trees. You might want to check it out."

She opened the side door. "Oh, I almost forgot," she said with twinkling eyes. "Some people think his ghost hangs around there, looking for his children. So keep your eyes open!" With that, she went inside.

The kids found a path through the trees. As they walked, Dink told Josh and Ruth Rose what Wallis had said on the beach.

"So it *is* a ghost!" Josh said. "Creepy!"

"No way," Ruth Rose said. "I don't believe in ghosts. It must be an animal trapped somewhere in the castle."

"I don't know," Dink said. "Wallis told me she searched the whole place."

"Besides," said Josh, "what kind of animal makes a spooky scream like that?"

Just then the kids reached the playhouse. The outside of the small wooden building had been painted to look like Wallis's castle. A kid-sized drawbridge crossed a shallow moat to the front door.

"Excellent," said Josh.

"Let's go inside!" Ruth Rose cried, running to the door. She tugged on the handle, and the door opened with a soft whoosh.

Ruth Rose curtsied. "Enter, my loyal knights!"

"His Highness King Dink goes first," Dink said, nudging ahead of Josh.

They crowded into the room. Everything was covered with a layer of dust. Dim light shone through two small windows covered with cobwebs.

Josh rubbed his arms. "Boy, this place is cold," he said.

"Looks like no one's been in here for years," Ruth Rose said.

A round table and two little chairs stood in the middle of the room on a dusty, worn rug. A shelf held a miniature set of blue dishes. Under the shelf, a lonely-looking teddy bear sat on an old sofa.

"This place creeps me out," Josh said.

"Look," Dink said. "Footprints on the rug." He stepped into one of them. "Whoever made these sure has big feet!"

"Do ghosts leave footprints?" Josh asked.

"Maybe it's Walker," Ruth Rose suggested. "They're too big to be Wallis's."

"But why would Walker come here?" Dink wondered out loud.

"Can we go?" Josh pleaded. "I just saw a monster spider, and he was looking back at me!"

"Okay, but let's come back," Ruth Rose said. "I want to clean this place. It's sad to see it all dusty like this."

Ruth Rose pulled the door shut behind them. As they crossed the draw-bridge, Dink noticed something in the moat. He jumped down and picked up a bright green feather.

"Hey, guys, look! It's like the one that was stuck to Josh's sneaker."

Ruth Rose held the feather up to the sun. "What's it from?"

Josh examined the feather. "The only bird I know with this kind of feather is a parrot," he said. "But parrots don't live in Maine."

Dink took the feather back from

Josh, then put it in his pocket.

"Okay, we've explored the play-house," Josh said. "Now you guys have to do what I want."

Dink grinned at his friend. "You mean eat?"

"No. I want to check out that cave down on the beach."

"Wait a minute," Dink said. "You were creeped out by the playhouse, but you want to explore the cave?"

"Caves are cool," Josh said. "Come on, you guys."

The kids headed past the castle, through the gate, and down the cliff. They stood looking at the small river flowing out of the cave. "I wonder how deep it is," Dink said.

"There's one way to find out," Josh said. He stepped in the water and began wading into the cave. The water reached just above his ankles.

"Come on, you guys!" he called over his shoulder.

Dink and Ruth Rose followed him. The cave grew darker, until the sunlight disappeared. The air was cold and damp, and the black walls felt slimy.

"Josh, this water is freezing," Ruth Rose said. Her voice sounded hollow. "I hate it in here! Can we go back?"

"The water's getting deeper, too," Dink said. "And I can't even see you guys!"

"Shh!" Josh said. "I heard something!"

"Josh, don't try to scare us!" Ruth Rose said. "I'm already—"

Suddenly a scream echoed through the cave.

"RUN!" Ruth Rose yelled.

Over their heads, hundreds of black bats streaked for daylight.

Chapter 5

The kids didn't stop running till they were at the top of the cliff. Dink threw himself on the ground, trying to catch his breath.

"What was that?" Ruth Rose asked, pulling off her sopping sneakers. "My heart nearly stopped!"

"It was the ghost!" Josh said. "I bet that cave leads to a secret dungeon under the castle. Maybe that's where Emory Scott died!"

Ruth Rose burst out laughing. Josh ignored her. "There must be a secret door leading to the dungeon some-where. And I'm going to find it!"

"Maybe you are," Dink said. "But *I'm* gonna take a shower and change."

"Me too," Ruth Rose said. "I smell like a fish!"

When they got back to the castle, Walker's Jeep was parked out front. The kids cleaned up, then hurried down to the kitchen. Wallis, Walker, and Rip were sitting at the long table, husking ears of corn.

"Hi, kids," Walker said. "How was your first day at Moose Manor?"

"It was great," Josh said, shooting Dink a look. "We explored the play-

house and found some neat stuff on the beach."

Dink figured Josh wanted to keep his "secret dungeon" idea to himself.

"Well, I have lobsters to cook," Wallis said. "I hope everyone's hungry!"

After supper, the grownups decided to play Scrabble.

"You kids can join us," Wallis said. "Or you can choose another board game from the hall closet. Help yourself."

"Um...I think I'll go upstairs and read," Josh said. He motioned for Dink and Ruth Rose to follow him. They met upstairs in the hall between the bedrooms. "Let's search up here while they're playing Scrabble," he said.

"What exactly are we looking for?" Dink asked.

"A secret door or passageway," Josh

said, rapping his knuckle lightly on a wall.

"Josh, don't you think Wallis would've told us about a secret door?" Ruth Rose said.

"Maybe she doesn't know about it," Josh said.

"I guess we should look around," Dink agreed. *"Something* is making those weird noises."

"Let's start on the roof," Ruth Rose said.

They walked down the hall, and Josh pushed open the narrow door.

At the top of the stairs, they opened another door. A cool breeze blew in their faces as they stepped onto the flat roof.

"Wow! You can see everything!" said Josh. "It would be neat to fly a kite up here!"

Dink stood between two granite

battlements that were taller than he was. He felt like a king looking over his land.

"There's nothing up here," Josh said.

"Okay," Dink said. "Let's look downstairs."

The kids tromped back down to the hall.

Ruth Rose walked into her room while Dink and Josh searched theirs. Dink started with the closet, but found only dust and an old tennis racket.

He used the racket to poke behind the window curtains. A few spiders darted away, but nothing else.

Suddenly Josh screamed from the bathroom. "Dink, it's got me! Help!"

Dink charged into the bathroom, holding the tennis racket like a club. He looked around wildly, but the room was empty.

"Josh? Where are you?"

The shower curtain flew open. Josh stood there, grinning. "Boo!"

Dink shook his head. "You're so lame, Josh. It would serve you right if some ghost did get you!"

Josh climbed out of the tub. "Thought you didn't believe in ghosts, Dinkus!"

Dink just shook his head again. He crossed the hall and knocked on Ruth Rose's door. "Find anything?" he asked.

She shook her head. "Nope."

She and Dink searched the long hall. They looked behind the radiators and inside plant pots and one tall umbrella stand.

Josh tapped on the walls, listening for hollow sounds. Finally they gave up, sweaty and dusty.

"I don't know where else to search," Dink said.

"We didn't check out the downstairs rooms," Josh said.

"We'll have to wait till tomorrow," Ruth Rose said, yawning. "I'm going to bed. And I hope I don't dream about ghosts, thanks to Josh Pinto!"

Josh grinned. "I read somewhere that ghosts eat girls with curls."

"Just let one try!" she said, then slammed her door.

Dink and Josh climbed into bed. A few minutes later they were both asleep.

Dink woke suddenly, his heart thumping. He looked at the clock. It was midnight!

Dink climbed out of bed and tiptoed to the window. He saw black trees against a blacker sky.

Then he saw it—a ghostly light near the playhouse!

Chapter 6

Dink gulped and felt goose bumps climbing his legs. Could it be Emory Scott's ghost?

The light winked a few more times, then disappeared.

Dink shivered, rubbing his eyes. When the light didn't return, he crawled back into bed.

He yawned and closed his eyes, deciding that he had seen a firefly.

But just before falling off to sleep, Dink opened his eyes again. He had seen only one light moving out there in the darkness.

Why would there be only one firefly in the woods? He thought about that until he fell asleep.

Dink dreamed that he was in the cave again. It was pitch dark. Up ahead, he heard a hideous scream. But this time, the scream didn't stop, it just got louder. Suddenly bats were flying in his face. But these bats had feathers—bright green feathers!

Dink bolted upright in his bed. The blankets were twisted around his legs and the alarm clock was buzzing.

I'm not in a cave, Dink realized. I'm still in the castle. Relieved, he shut off the alarm.

"Josh, wake up," he said.

Josh opened an eye. "Why?"

Dink climbed out of bed. "Walker's taking us lobstering, remember?" He turned on the light and yanked Josh's covers off.

"Come on, let's go catch a lobster!"

Josh groaned, but he climbed out of bed. "I hate lobsters."

Dink laughed. "You ate one last night." He pulled on yesterday's jeans and a warm sweatshirt over his T-shirt. "I'm going downstairs. Don't go back to bed!"

Dink crossed the hall and tapped on Ruth Rose's door. She was up and dressed in yellow from top to bottom.

"Did you see anything strange last night?" Dink asked.

Ruth Rose was pulling a brush through her hair. She shook her head.

"Well, I did! I'll tell you about it downstairs."

There was a light on in the kitchen. Dink saw juice glasses, cereal bowls, and some muffins on the table. He was munching when Ruth Rose and Josh came in.

"Guys, I think someone was creeping around outside last night," Dink said. He told them about the light he'd seen in the woods.

Josh grabbed a muffin and bit off half.

"Told you," he said, trying to grin and chew at the same time. "It was Emory's ghost!"

"Very funny, Josh," Ruth Rose said.

Just then there was a thump in the mud room and the kitchen door crashed open. Josh nearly fell out of his chair.

Walker came in wearing tall rubber boots and a yellow slicker. "Ready to go?" he asked.

Dink laughed in relief. "Josh thought you were a ghost," he said.

"Did not," Josh muttered.

They walked outside and climbed into Walker's Jeep. The sky was pitch black. Dink peered into the woods, half expecting to see the strange light again.

A few minutes later Walker turned into his driveway. They got out and walked behind the house to the dock. Their feet made hollow noises on the wooden boards.

"Watch your step out here," Walker said, aiming a flashlight at Dink's feet.

Dink breathed in the salty night air. A few stars made pinpoints of light above the boat. Somewhere, he heard a night bird call.

"Ready to come aboard?" Walker asked.

Dink, Josh, and Ruth Rose followed Walker onto the dark boat.

Chapter 7

"Better slip one of those on," Walker said when they were aboard. He pointed at orange life jackets hanging on a row of pegs.

The kids climbed into the bulky vests and sat on benches. Walker started the motor, and the small boat moved away from the dock.

"It'll be about an hour before we get to my pots," Walker hollered over the roar of the engine. "Get comfortable!"

Ruth Rose and Josh curled up on the benches, but Dink sat up. He didn't

want to miss a thing. He could smell
the lobster bait. Waves slapped against
the hull as they chugged through the
black water.

Dink watched the glow of morning
color the horizon pale yellow. It made
him remember the light he'd seen last
night. Did the light have anything to do
with the strange noises or the two green
feathers?

The boat's gentle rocking made
Dink feel sleepy. He closed his eyes.
Then Walker was shaking him. Dink sat
up and squinted into sunlight.

The waves rocked the boat back and
forth. When Dink stood, he nearly lost
his balance. "Where are we?" he asked.

"About five miles out," Walker said.
"Wake up Ruth Rose and Josh, and
we'll eat."

They sat in a patch of sunlight.
Breakfast was peanut butter sandwich-

es and hot, milky cocoa from Walker's thermos.

Dink saw other boats in the distance. "Are those all lobster boats?"

Walker nodded. "Most of them are. A few fishing boats are out, too."

Josh looked over the side. "How do you catch the lobsters?" he asked.

Walker pointed to a machine. "That winch brings them up. I'll show you how it works."

Walker picked up a long pole with a hook on one end. He used it to grab the rope attached to a marker buoy. He snagged the rope onto the winch, pushed a button, and wet rope began whistling up out of the water. Fast!

A few seconds later a lobster pot surfaced on the other end of the rope. Wearing a rubber apron and gloves, Walker dragged it into the boat.

The wooden trap was covered with

seaweed. A few small crabs scampered out onto the deck. "Let's see what we've got," Walker said, dropping the crabs back into the sea.

Walker opened the pot's small door and reached in a gloved hand. He pulled out a wet, dark green lobster. The lobster waved its claws angrily.

"Those claws can break a finger," Walker warned. He snapped two thick rubber bands onto the lobster's front claws. Then he dropped the lobster into a tank of sea water.

"Josh, get the bait, will you?"

Josh dragged the heavy pail over. Walker pulled out a huge fish head.

"Oh, phew!" Josh said. "That's gross!"

"The lobsters don't mind," Walker said, dropping the fish head into the lobster pot. He fastened the door and shoved the trap back into the water.

"That's pretty much how it's done," Walker said, slapping water off his gloves.

"Can we pull another one?" Dink asked.

"Sure, and you guys can help. Grab some gloves out of that locker."

Ruth Rose brought out three pairs of

thick rubber gloves. Walker winched up another pot and held a wiggling lobster out to Josh.

"Hold him by the back so he can't reach you with his claws."

Josh held the lobster with both gloved hands. Ruth Rose and Dink snapped rubber bands onto the claws.

"Who wants to put bait in the pot?" Walker asked, grinning.

Dink volunteered while Josh faked gagging noises. Dink stuck his hand into the bait bucket, then dropped a bloody fish head into the lobster pot.

The morning grew warm, so the kids stripped off their sweatshirts. The ocean was calm. Sea gulls soared overhead, watching for scraps.

"Look, there's Rip," Walker said.

Rip pulled his boat up next to *Lady Luck*. When the boats were side by side, Rip tossed a line to Dink.

"How's it going?" Rip asked. He was wearing clean jeans and a T-shirt. He held a coffee mug in one hand.

"We got a few," Walker said. "My crew here was a big help."

"Are you going lobstering?" Josh asked.

Rip shook his head and flashed a grin. "Not today, kiddo. Just came out to check my buoys. Toss me the line, okay?"

Dink tossed his end of the rope toward the other boat. Rip caught it in his free hand. "Have a good day!" he yelled as he pulled away.

"Anyone want more cocoa?" Walker asked.

"I do," Josh said.

Dink turned around and saw something on *Lady Luck*'s deck.

It was a bright green feather.

Chapter 8

Dink snatched up the feather. Ruth Rose raised her eyebrows. Dink shrugged and stuck the feather in his pocket.

"Ready to head in?" Walker asked. "I promised Sis I'd get you back before lunch."

He started up the engine, and they chugged toward land.

Back at Walker's dock, the kids helped him hose fish goo and seaweed off the deck of his boat. Then he drove them to the castle.

"Sis's car is gone," Walker said. "She must be out doing errands. Will you kids be okay for a while?"

"I'm a little hungry," Josh said, grinning.

"Here, finish this." Walker handed Josh the bread, peanut butter, and knife. He waved and drove away.

"Where should we eat?" Josh asked.

"How about the playhouse?" Ruth Rose said. "I can wash those little dishes." She found a watering can next to the mud room door and filled it from the spigot.

On the way to the playhouse, Dink pulled the feathers out of his pocket. He told Josh how he'd found the third one on Walker's boat.

The kids studied the feathers, holding them up to the sunlight. "They're exactly alike," Josh said.

"Another parrot feather?" Ruth Rose

asked. "Where could they be coming from?"

Josh grinned. "From a parrot?"

"Very funny, Joshua!"

Dink suddenly remembered his dream. Screaming bats with green feathers...

Ruth Rose opened the playhouse door and they walked in.

"It's too cold in here," Josh said. "Why don't we eat out in the sun?"

Dink helped Josh carry the table out.

Ruth Rose brought out the dishes and set them in the grass.

"The rug looks pretty dusty," Dink said. "We should drag it outside and sweep it."

Josh was spreading peanut butter on bread at the table. "Can we eat first, then work? My stomach is talking to me."

On his knees, Dink began rolling up the rug. "Your stomach is—hey, guys, look!"

"Not another green feather, I hope," Josh muttered. He strolled over to see.

Dink pointed to a trapdoor in the floor.

"Yes!" Josh yelled. "I told you! The secret door to the secret dungeon!"

Ruth Rose ran over. "Let's open it!" she said.

The handle had a spring lock. Ruth Rose squeezed the spring, and the lock popped open. With all three of them pulling, they were able to raise the trapdoor. They heard a creepy whoosh, then cold, damp air escaped.

"Yuck, what a smell!" Josh said.

The kids stared into the musty-smelling hole. Stone steps led down to darkness. Even in the dim light, they saw footprints on the steps.

"Just like the prints we saw on the rug," Dink said.

They all jumped back as a hollow scream echoed out of the dark hole.

Chapter 9

"Something's down there!" Ruth Rose whispered.

Josh's eyes were huge. "Not some-*thing*," he whispered. "Some*one*. It's the ghost of Emory Scott!"

Dink put his hand in his pocket and felt the three green parrot feathers.

Taking a deep breath, he put a foot on the top step. "I'm going down," he said.

Dink walked down the steps, feeling along the cold stone walls. He tried not to think about slimy things that hung out in damp tunnels.

Then his hand touched something square and hard. A light switch! He flipped it up, and the space was suddenly flooded with light.

"It's a long tunnel!" he yelled.

Ruth Rose hurried down the steps. She turned to Josh. "Coming?"

"All right," Josh sighed. "But if anything touches me, I'm out of here!"

The tunnel was cold and narrow. They walked along the dirt floor. Small, cobweb-covered light bulbs hung from the ceiling. The air smelled rotten.

The tunnel went straight for a while, then turned a corner.

"Listen," Ruth Rose said. "I hear water."

"I hate this," Josh said. "I really do."

Dink turned the corner and found himself standing in water. Something let out a screech, and Dink froze.

Josh grabbed Dink around the neck.

"What the heck was that?" he squeaked.

"Josh, you're strangling me!" Dink croaked.

"Sorry," Josh said.

"Where are we?" Ruth Rose asked.

They were standing at the entrance to a cave. The rock walls oozed, and the floor was under water. Off to the left, another tunnel continued out of sight.

"I think I know where we are," Dink whispered.

"Me too," Josh said. "We're in the dungeon. I'd better not see any skeletons!"

"I think if we'd kept going through the cave yesterday," Dink continued, "we'd have ended up here."

"It's one long tunnel," Ruth Rose said. "From the playhouse to the ocean!"

Then something behind them made a loud squawk.

Josh jumped, nearly knocking Dink over.

"Look, guys," Ruth Rose said. "Over there!" She pointed to a dark mound up against one wall.

Dink walked over, splashing through the cold water.

"It's a tarp," he said.

Holding his breath, Dink grabbed one corner and yanked it away. Under the tarp were two cages, one on top of the other. Each cage held four large green parrots.

The birds panicked, beating their wings against the cage bars. Their screams echoed again and again off the cave walls.

"So much for the ghost of Emory Scott," Ruth Rose said.

Josh laughed. "Good! I don't know what I'd have done if I'd bumped into him!"

Dink pulled the feathers from his pocket. He held them next to one of the parrots.

"They're the same," he said.

"What the heck *is* this place?" Ruth Rose asked. "Who'd hide parrots in a cave?"

"I don't know," Dink said.

"Guys!" Ruth Rose said. She was looking down. "The tide must be coming in. The water is getting deeper!"

Dink and Josh looked down. The water was up to their ankles!

"The parrots!" Josh said.

The bottom cage was getting wet. The parrots shrieked at the rising water.

"Let's get them outside!" Dink said, grabbing the top cage. He lugged it into the dry tunnel.

Josh and Ruth Rose took the other cage. They hurried back along the tunnel with the parrots squawking in fear.

Dink stopped at the bottom of the stone steps and looked up. "Uh-oh."

"What?" Ruth Rose gasped.

"I thought we left the trapdoor open," Dink said.

"We did," Josh said.

"Well, it's closed now." Dink set his cage on the floor. He walked up the steps and pushed on the door. It didn't budge.

Josh climbed the steps, and they both shoved against the door.

"It's no use," Dink said. "The door must have fallen, and the lock snapped shut."

"What can we do?" Ruth Rose asked. "If the tide floods this tunnel..."

Dink walked back down the steps. "There's another way out. But we'll have to swim."

Chapter 10

"Where?" Ruth Rose asked.

"We can go back to the cave and swim out through the tunnel," Dink explained.

"But there are bats in there!"

"It's our only way out," Josh said.

The kids lugged the two cages back through the tunnel. The parrots screeched and beat their wings.

In the cave, the water was almost up to their knees, and rising.

"We better get out of here fast," Josh said.

Ruth Rose peered into the other tunnel. "I wonder how far it is to the beach," she said.

"It can't be that far," Dink said. "We're probably right under the castle."

"How are we gonna swim and carry these cages at the same time?" Josh asked. He glanced around the dark cave. "We need a raft or something."

"If the water's not too deep, we can walk out," Dink said.

He handed his cage to Ruth Rose, then stepped into the deeper water. It came up to his waist.

"It's kind of cold," he said, shivering, "but it's not very deep. We can carry the cages out."

"But what if it gets deeper?" Josh asked. "We can't carry the cages on our heads!"

"I have an idea," Ruth Rose said. "I read it in a Girl Scout magazine. It showed how to use your jeans as floats. You can make water wings by tying knots in the ankles and legs."

"You mean get undressed?" Josh said. "No way!"

"That's a great idea," Dink said. He climbed back out of the deep water, then kicked out of his sneakers and wet jeans. He tied knots in his jeans and put his sneakers back on.

Dink looked at Josh. "Come on," he said. "The water's getting deeper."

"Okay, but I feel weird," Josh muttered, pulling off his sneakers and jeans. The water reached just below his boxer shorts.

Dink tied knots in Josh's jeans, then dropped both pairs into the water. The air-filled jeans floated!

"Ready?" Dink said. They stepped into the water and balanced the two cages on top of the floating jeans.

"It works!" said Ruth Rose.

"This water's cold and yucky," Josh said.

"At least we can touch bottom," Dink said. "Okay, let's go."

The tunnel grew darker as they waded away from the cave. The water reached their chests, but got no higher.

The parrots were quiet, as if they knew they were being rescued.

"Do you think there are sharks in here?" Josh said. His voice echoed.

"No," Dink said. "Just a few man-eating lobsters."

Suddenly they heard a whispery sound in the darkness around them.

"What's that?" Ruth Rose asked.

"Calm down," Josh said, giggling. "It's just bats. We must've scared them."

"Are they friendly?" asked Ruth Rose.

"Not if you're an insect," Josh said.

Finally they saw daylight. Ahead was the ocean end of the tunnel.

"We did it, guys!" Dink said. They dragged the cages and soggy jeans to the beach near where they'd eaten their picnic.

"Boy, does the sun feel good!" Josh said, flopping down on the sand.

The kids rested and caught their

breath. Dink and Josh took the knots out of their jeans and spread them out to dry.

"I was thinking about these parrots," Josh said. "I have a book about endangered birds, and I think these guys are in it."

"Why would anyone hide endangered parrots in a cave?" Ruth Rose asked.

"Poachers," Josh said, pulling off his soaked sneakers. "Poachers catch rare animals and sell them for a lot of money."

"But who?"

Josh shrugged. "Someone who knows about the tunnel."

"I think I know who it is," Dink said.

Josh and Ruth Rose looked at him.

"Who?" Josh asked.

Dink looked sad. "Walker Wallace."

Chapter 11

"WHAT?" Ruth Rose yelled. "That's crazy!"

Dink shrugged. "I found one of the feathers in his Jeep and another on his boat."

Josh nodded slowly. "And when we had our picnic here yesterday, Wallis said Walker had been in the cave. Maybe he found the trapdoor in the playhouse."

"The footprints on the rug were big enough to be his," Dink said.

Ruth Rose stood up and wiped sand

off her wet jeans. "I don't believe you guys. Walker wouldn't break the law! And he sure wouldn't use his sister's house!"

"I hope not," Dink said. "Anyway, let's get the parrots up to the castle."

Dink and Josh tugged on their damp jeans and grabbed the cages. A few minutes later they burst into Wallis's kitchen.

She was writing at the table.

"We found out what's making those noises!" Dink blurted out.

The kids told Wallis about the tunnel to the cave and the parrots.

"A trapdoor in the playhouse!" Wallis exclaimed with wide eyes. "And a tunnel? How incredible!"

"It's like a secret passageway," Josh said. "Maybe pirates hid gold down there!"

"Well, I don't know about pirates,"

Wallis said. "But now I know how Emory Scott got all that marble and stuff up here!"

"What should we do with the parrots?" asked Ruth Rose.

"Show me," Wallis said.

They all trooped into the mud room. When the door opened, the parrots began flapping around in the cages. Their shrieks filled the room.

"Poor things," Wallis said. "Should we feed them? What do parrots eat?"

"Got any fruit?" Josh said. "That's what they'd eat in the rain forests."

Wallis went to the kitchen.

"I wonder where these guys came from," said Ruth Rose.

Josh studied the parrots. "Probably Africa or South America," he said.

"How would the poachers get them all the way to Maine?" Dink asked.

"By boat," Josh said. "Then a smaller

boat would bring them into the cave."

"A boat like Walk—"

Dink stopped talking as Wallis came back with two peeled bananas and a bunch of grapes. They dropped the fruit into the cages. The parrots grabbed the food in their beaks.

"They were starving!" Wallis said. She placed a bowl of water in each cage.

"I'm kind of hungry, too," Josh said. "We missed lunch."

"Well, we can't have that!" Wallis said. "Come into the kitchen."

While she made sandwiches, Dink explained about the light he'd seen in the woods the night before. "I bet there were more cages. They must take them out through the playhouse at night."

"We should hide down there and see who it is!" Ruth Rose said.

Wallis shook her head. "Absolutely

not. Those people could be dangerous!"

She brought out plates and napkins. "Today is Sunday, but tomorrow morning I'm going to call the state capitol. They must have someone who deals with poachers."

Wallis looked at the kids. "Promise me you'll stay out of that tunnel and cave."

Dink kicked Ruth Rose and Josh under the table.

"We promise," he said.

After lunch, the kids went back to the playhouse. They cleaned the dishes and swept the rug.

"I wish we could get these poacher guys," Dink said.

"I think we should sleep in the playhouse," Josh said. "Then if anyone comes, we'll grab them!"

"Josh, they'd grab *us* and stick us in

a cage," Ruth Rose said.

"Besides, Wallis would never let us stay down here," Dink said. "But I have another idea!"

At one-thirty in the morning, the kids were crouched by the window in Dink and Josh's dark room. They were fully dressed.

Josh yawned. "Maybe no one is coming tonight."

"Maybe they know we found the cages," Dink said. "Walker could've seen us from his boat."

"I still don't think it's Walker," Ruth Rose said. "But whoever it is will have to come to feed the parrots, right?"

"Right," Dink said. "Let's take turns watching. I'll go first. You guys can snooze."

"Wake me up if you see any bad guys!" Josh said, flopping on his bed.

"Well, I'm not tired," Ruth Rose said. "I hope they go to jail for a hundred years!"

She and Dink stared out into the darkness. The alarm clock counted away the minutes.

Josh began snoring.

"Look," Ruth Rose whispered a while later. "A firefly."

Dink saw a light moving slowly through the darkness. "Wake Josh," he told her. "That's no lightning bug!"

The kids tiptoed past Wallis's room, then hurried down the steps and out through the mud room door. Creeping silently, they approached the playhouse.

Moonlight fell on the clearing. A few yards from the playhouse, a dark car stood in the shadows.

Dink grabbed Josh and Ruth Rose and pointed. It was Walker's Jeep!

"I guess you were right," Ruth Rose whispered sadly.

The kids inched forward. Suddenly Dink saw a light coming from the playhouse.

A man was bent over, pulling open the trapdoor! A glowing flashlight lay on the floor next to his feet.

The man stood up. In the flashlight's beam, Dink recognized who it was.

Ruth Rose grabbed his arm. "Ripley Pearce!" she whispered.

A moment later, Rip disappeared down the steps into the tunnel.

Suddenly Josh bolted around the corner of the playhouse and through the open door.

Before Dink could say anything, Josh slammed the trapdoor shut. Dink heard the spring lock snap into place.

Chapter 12

"What's Operation Game Thief?" Dink asked the next day.

"It's an 800 number you can call in Maine to report poachers," Wallis explained. She brought more hot pancakes to the table.

No one had gotten much sleep. After locking the trapdoor, Dink, Josh, and Ruth Rose had run back to wake up Wallis. She'd called 911 and reported poachers on her property.

The police had come and arrested Rip. The officers gave Wallis the Operation Game Thief phone number.

Wallis had then driven Walker's Jeep to his house and brought him back to the castle.

"The Maine Fish and Game Department will have plenty of questions for Rip," Walker said. "Trading in endangered animals is a federal crime."

"How did Rip get the parrots?" Josh asked.

"He must have contacts in the countries where they were captured," Walker said. "The police will be checking his phone bills to see whom he called."

"He probably used his own lobster boat," Wallis said, shaking her head. "No wonder it always looked so clean."

"Why did he have your Jeep?" Josh asked.

Walker speared another pancake. "Rip's car conked out a few days ago, so I let him borrow mine."

"It was a perfect set-up," Wallis said. "Rip needed money, and he had contacts who would pay a lot for rare parrots."

"I wonder if he sold any other animals," Josh said, "like monkeys or snakes."

"We may find out yet," Walker said. He winked at Josh. "What made you decide to shut the trapdoor on Rip?"

"I got mad!" Josh said. "I wanted him to see how it felt to be in a cage."

"So that green feather on Josh's sneaker came from Rip, right?" Dink asked.

Walker nodded. "He probably brought it into the Jeep on his foot. And the one you found on my boat got there the same way."

Josh blushed. "For a while we thought you were the poacher," he told Walker.

"Well, *I* never did!" Ruth Rose said.

Walker grinned at Ruth Rose. "Thanks! What made you so sure?"

"You're too busy," she answered. "And you wouldn't be mean to parrots. You threw those little crabs back in the water yesterday."

"What will happen to the parrots?" Dink asked.

"I assume they'll go back to where they came from," Walker said. "And Rip will most likely go to jail."

"And thanks to you kids, I won't have to hear any more strange noises," Wallis said.

She grinned shyly. "But to tell the truth, I think I'll miss the ghost of Emory Scott. I kind of liked living in a haunted castle!"

Just then a loud screech came from the mud room.

HAVE YOU READ ALL THE BOOKS IN THE

A to Z Mysteries®

SERIES?

Help Dink, Josh, and Ruth Rose . . .

...solve mysteries from A to Z!

Turn the page
for a sneak peek at

A to Z Mysteries®

SUPER EDITION 1

DETECTIVE CAMP

BY
RON ROY

Available now!

CHAPTER 1

"Here y'are, kids," the taxi driver told Dink, Josh, and Ruth Rose. "Get out and stretch your legs and I'll fetch your luggage."

The kids stepped out of the taxi in Bear Walk, Vermont. They were standing next to a gravel driveway in front of an old lodge built of timber. A banner over the wide porch said WELCOME TO DETECTIVE CAMP.

Behind the lodge stood a red barn with its doors open wide.

Dink noticed a few picnic tables on the lawn between the lodge and the barn. Across from the driveway stood three log cabins surrounded by wildflowers, shrubs, and trees. Off to the side of the cabins stood a larger building. Dink noticed a sign that said WASH-HOUSE. White arrows pointed boys to one door and girls to another.

"Where are we supposed to sleep?" Josh asked. Like Dink, he wore cutoff jean shorts and a T-shirt.

"Didn't you read the letter?" Dink asked, winking at Ruth Rose. "Josh Pinto sleeps in a bear cave." Dink's full name was Donald David Duncan, but his friends called him Dink.

Josh didn't say anything, but he made a goofy face at Dink.

"In those cabins, I guess," said Ruth Rose, pointing. "I see some other kids over there." Ruth Rose liked to dress all in one color. Today she wore pink from her headband to her sneakers.

"Tell me again why we're in Bear Walk, Vermont," Josh said, glancing around. "I'll bet there are bears everywhere!"

"We came to Detective Camp because we love solving mysteries," Ruth Rose said. "Besides, none of us has been to sleepaway camp before. It'll be fun! We'll learn all about—"

"Yo!" someone yelled. The kids looked toward the cabins. Three teenagers were walking toward them. They each wore a white T-shirt with DETECTIVE CAMP on the front and green shorts. Whistles hung from lanyards around their necks.

"Are you the kids from Green Lawn, Connecticut?" a tall boy with a buzz cut asked.

"Yes," Dink said. "I'm Dink, and these

are my friends Josh and Ruth Rose."

"I'm Buzzy Steele," the boy said, smiling. "You two guys are in my cabin, the one with the moose over the door."

"And I'm Angie Doe," the girl said. She had red hair in pigtails. "Ruth Rose, you're in Fox Cabin with me. You'll have nine roommates!"

The other boy had broad shoulders and dark skin. "I'm Lucas Washington," he said. "Call me Luke. I have Bear Cabin with eight more guys."

"How many kids are here altogether?" Dink asked.

"Twenty-six," Angie said. "Sixteen boys and ten girls."

The taxi driver handed the kids' packs and sleeping bags to them. "Have a good time," he said, getting back into the taxi. Then he turned the cab around and pulled away.

"Let's get you kids into your cabins,"

Luke said, reaching for an armful of sleeping bags. "Everyone else got here this morning."

They followed the three counselors onto the lawn. Stone paths led up to each of the three small porches.

"After you get unpacked, we're all meeting down by Shady Lake," Angie told the kids. "About twenty minutes, okay? Just follow that path, and the lake will be right in front of you. Ready to meet your cabinmates, Ruth Rose?"

"Yes!" Ruth Rose said. "See you later, guys." She followed Angie into a cabin with a wooden cutout of a fox over the door.

"Later," Luke said. He loped next door.

Buzzy led Dink and Josh through a door with a moose cutout over it. Inside the cabin, six boys were reading and playing board games. A shelf in one corner was overflowing with books and games.

Dink counted four sets of bunk beds. Near the door was a single bed. Dink assumed that was where Buzzy would sleep.

"Yo, guys, listen up!" Buzzy yelled.

"Come and meet Dink and Josh from Connecticut."

Six boys turned toward Dink and Josh. They smiled and, one by one, introduced themselves and shook hands.

Dink tried to remember the six new names and faces: A black-haired boy

named Billy Wong. A thin kid with braces called Hunter. Ian and Brendan, twins with blond hair so light it appeared white. Duke, a tall boy. And Campbell, a short blond kid with a big smile.

"If you need to wash up or use the bathroom, that's all in the big building on the other side of Fox Cabin," Buzzy told the boys.

"We have to go outside to the bathroom?" Josh asked.

Buzzy nodded. "Yep. The showers are there, too," he said. "And don't let the hot water run too long, or someone gets a cold shower! You all need to be down at Shady Lake in about ten minutes, okay?"

"Are we going swimming?" Hunter asked. "Are there snakes in the water?"

"No and yes," Buzzy said, grinning. "There are a few harmless water snakes, but we're not going swimming today. We're just having a meeting with all the other campers."

Dink and Josh headed for the only set of bunks not piled up with the other kids' stuff.

"I guess this one is ours," Dink said. "Top or bottom?"

"Top," Josh said, tossing his sleeping bag up onto the mattress. "That way, if a bear comes in, he gets you first."

Dink grinned. "Bears can climb, Josh," he said.

"I'll still take the top bunk," Josh said. He grabbed his backpack and climbed the ladder.

Dink unrolled his sleeping bag and fluffed up the pillow he found on his mattress. As he emptied his backpack, he glanced out the window just over his bed. He could see a wooden fence separating the lawn from deep woods.

He arranged his clothes in a cubby that already had his name on it. He set his toothbrush and other toilet articles on the windowsill. He'd brought a couple of books, which he stood next to his toothpaste. The titles were *Wild Animals of Vermont* and *Danny Doon, Boy Detective.*

Josh was on top, wrestling with his sleeping bag.

"Are you ready?" Dink asked.

"Almost," Josh said. "My brothers used this sleeping bag last, and they tied about a million knots in the string."

"Okay, let's hustle," Buzzy called out. "Moose Cabin is never late! Now let's go, little moosies!"

The other six boys stampeded out the cabin door and raced for the path that led to the lake. A minute later, Buzzy followed them.

Dink waited for Josh on the porch.

Josh snuck up behind Dink and said, "Come back inside. I want to show you something."

"What?" Dink said as he followed Josh. "Come on, we're gonna be late on our first day!"

"Look," Josh said. He was pointing to a small wooden chest under Buzzy's bed. It had a hasp, and the padlock was in the locked position.

"Josh, what do I care if—"

"After the other kids left, I saw Buzzy hide something in there," Josh said. "He was real careful, like he didn't want anyone to see what he was doing."

"But Josh the snoop saw him, right?" Dink asked.

Josh nodded. "This is Detective Camp, right?" he said. "Well, I'm being a detective!"

Collect clues with
Dink, Josh, and Ruth Rose
in their next exciting
adventure!

THE
EMPTY
ENVELOPE

The kids peered over the hedge. A
man and a woman got out of the car.
The man was short and was wearing a
green suit and a purple tie.

"That's him!" Josh whispered. "The
guy who was following us before!"

The kids watched the man and the
woman talk for a few minutes, then
get back into the car. But they didn't
drive away.

"What the heck are they doing?"
Josh asked.

Dink gulped. He put his hand over
the envelope hidden under his shirt.

"They're waiting for me," he said.